HITLER WAS MY
MOTHER-IN-LAW

Six years of pure Hell, and I know only too well that I will never be permitted to escape—I know far too much about what is afoot in Hawsbortem Towers. It started soon after our marriage. After the initial onslaught on my body she soon tired of hitting me, and I discovered that she was taking many lovers. To my intense chagrin, one of the men she bedded was papa.

One rather gloomy Sunday evening, I was creeping round the house via my secret passage and found myself peering through a hole just above a portrait of Isaac Potts-Belching, the club-footed second baronet who lost his ear in a circular saw. Through the hole I squinted, and suddenly into view came Frau Gruber with six of her big blond relations. But caressing Frau Gruber was—Greta!

HITLER WAS MY MOTHER-IN-LAW

Les Dawson

ARROW BOOKS

Arrow Books Limited
17-21 Conway Street, London W1P 6JD

An imprint of the Hutchinson Publishing Group

London Melbourne Sydney Auckland
Johannesburg and agencies throughout
the world

Firsrt published by Robson Books Ltd 1982
Arrow edition 1985

© Les Dawson 1982

Printed and bound in Great Britain by
Anchor Brendon Limited, Tiptree, Essex

ISBN 0 09 940010 3

I have taken the liberty of including some comments on this book by people from divers walks of life.

'An education. It taught me a lesson.'

Mrs C., Wolverhampton

'A marvellous novel. For years I have suffered from insomnia, but after reading this story for only five minutes I couldn't keep my eyes open.'

The Very Reverend Pillfuddle

'Truly a load of cobblers.'

Shoe Repairers' Weekly

'What the book lacks in interest, it makes up for in dreariness.'

The Skipton Bugle

'My daddy rote it.'

Miss Pamela Dawson

March 15th

Dear Mr Dawson,

I saw you on the telly recently, and remembered seeing you on
Michael Parkinson. You'd told him that you had written a couple of
books, and were always on the lookout for unusual stories.

Well, I'm sending you the beginning of one.

When I was a patient in the Institution at Miresea-on-Crouch (after
I had a nervous breakdown) I met this nice gentleman who used to
play his flute for me. And, for a bit of fun, he used to chase me with
wads of cotton wool – I don't know what the game was about because
he never caught me. (Mike Parkinson isn't bent really, is he?)

I was the only one who bothered with this gentleman, who said his
name was Sir Peregrine Oswald Potts-Belching. All the other patients
kept away from him, and Dr Snow wouldn't go near him without a
rifle handy.

He told me a lot about his life, and he's written some of it down. It
was so good I decided to send it to you, hoping you'd give me a lot of
money.

I have been discharged from the Institution (though they say I can
go back whenever I want to), and I'm back at my old job in a
solicitor's. I work there as a teapot.

Yours sincerely ever,

Amy Pluckett (Miss)

Amy Pluckett (Miss)

After perusing the first part of the strange tale you are about to read, I went to see Miss Pluckett – sure enough, she's full of tea.

I stood outside the office of Fumbling and Bold, looking through the window, and watched this woman swallow two spoons of dry tea (one for herself, one for the pot), then take a long swig of boiling water. After a bit she stirred herself, and had a sip of milk and two spoons of sugar. I crept quietly away.

I visited the Institution, but Dr Snow would not allow me to be alone with the man who calls himself Sir Peregrine Oswald Potts-Belching. He said it was for my own safety...

Here, then, told by Amy Pluckett and Sir Peregrine Oswald Potts-Belching is:

Hitler Was My Mother-in-Law

THE STORY opens in 1948.

In the austere drawing room of Hawsbortem Towers—an ill-kempt chamber possessed of all the radiant charm usually associated with an Arab bedpan—Lady Julia Potts-Belching finally glanced up from her indifferent needlework. She fixed her husband with the sort of withering glare that would have blunted a Burmese machete, remarking acidly as she did so, 'Do stop prowling to and fro, Henry. You look like something out of the Big Top.'

Sir Henry Potts-Belching, sixth baronet, snorted like one of his own Suffolk Punches, threw his cigar butt into the empty maw of the huge fireplace, and trumpeted, 'Even you, Julia, must have realised by now that we are in dire straits—potential fodder for the social knacker's yard!'

At this, Lady Julia stiffened, ramrod fashion. 'Kindly moderate your language, Henry. We are not Liberals,' she replied spiritedly.

Sir Henry shook his shaggy mane, frustration clearly showing, and bellowed: 'Damn it, woman, we are penniless. Bereft of the filthy! Or, in the parlance of the village—skint! I warn you, it won't be long, my beauty, before some wretched Socialist in a red hat bungs us both a string bag full of biscuits and then totes us away to a prefabricated hostel where they drink beer and bat you with a Keir Hardie pamphlet.' He interrupted his impassioned diatribe as he caught sight of the cigar butt he'd just thrown away. He stooped and retrieved it from the grate, dusted it on the sleeve of his dog-eared smoking jacket and placed it tenderly in a tin that had once contained cough lozenges.

Lady Julia had lost interest in her husband's ranting, and had retreated into her own special world. She did not live in the present: hers was a realm of dashing Hussars, of dainty maidens who fainted in odd gazebos, of breathless confidences exchanged at point-to-point meetings and tea rooms in Harrogate. The war had passed Lady Julia by completely, and—apart from knitting a pair of socks for a submarine rating—she had scarcely acknowledged that it was happening.

Her wedding in the late 1930s to Sir Henry had been a grand affair. It had also caused vast amusement among the socialites of the day, principally because both families had given their approval to the match on the understanding that their respective ageing offspring would come into a worthwhile inheritance. Alas, Julia's father had squandered everything in South America, looking for El Dorado; and Henry's father, who had demeaned the family name but temporarily restored its fortunes by inventing—and marketing—the once-lucrative Potts-Belching Pith Helmet For Gentlemen, suddenly discovered that there were no longer enough fierce colonial types to sustain sales of his grotesque 'titfers'. (In fact, he went . . . strange, and ran away to sea with a draughtsman from Ormskirk.)

Over the years Hawsbortem Towers began to sag a little, and the cost of restoring the old pile was enough to turn the average aristocrat mauve. The servants had long ago fled the Towers at the vista of penury, and the staff left to man the tottering heap numbered but three: Albert, the footman (who stayed on because the stately home was off the beaten track, and he was therefore less likely to be apprehended for his bigamy and desertion in the Sudan), and two German women, Frau Gruber and her daughter Greta, who did all the cleaning and cooking. Sir Henry, then a Captain of Dragoons, had helped them escape the burning ashes of Berlin, smuggling them away from the ruined city and the Russians' grasp—in return for a promise of money from a Swiss bank account, and the daughter's willingness to share his bed.

For a time, the arrangement had worked like a dream. The formidable Frau Gruber had slipped Sir Henry enough cash to keep his top-knot above water; and from time to time—when he felt randy after a bout with the port—the daughter obliged him on a mattress in the West Wing.

But six months before our story opens, the cash-flow had turned into a drip and the amatory relationship had cooled. Sir Henry had confronted both women, but with little success; and on one occasion his bluster had been interrupted by two strange bulky men dressed in black leather. They had thrown the seething baronet into his own horse trough, and from that day things had seemed to go wrong. Two of his geldings, chestnuts, had been strangled in a thicket and he had found what looked like a scorched effigy of himself in a lavatory.

Finally, in desperation, Sir Henry had gone down on his knees to Frau Gruber, begging for salvation. Her price for the restoration of the Swiss money was simple: marriage between her daughter and Sir Henry's only son, Peregrine Oswald.

Common sense and the need for fresh meat reconciled the baronet to losing both his son and his regular crumpet. The boy was not the fruit of his union with Lady Julia, but the result of a romp with a dairymaid in a haywain, and—since she looked upon sex as a farmyard activity—Lady Julia had forgiven her husband his indiscretion, allowed the boy to be acknowledged and brought up as a Potts-Belching, then forgotten all about him and withdrawn into her own private world.

Peregrine Oswald was doomed from the outset. His father consigned him first to a triangular nanny with a faint moustache, and then to a tutor. Sir Henry had washed his hands of his son and either did not know or did not care that this tutor, Trevor, was a dreamy young man with a friend in the Royal Ballet and was drawing young Peregrine into a hazy limbo of books, poetry, chamber music and madrigals. When Trevor contracted rabies and was found dead in a culvert, Peregrine retreated into a shell furnished by his mentor's taste; gradually, the household had forgotten the wan youth in the library.

Sir Henry was surveying the scene from the mullioned window, but his mind was made up. Peregrine Oswald owed his father something; and saving Hawsbortem Towers was the only thing that mattered. He was no longer a boy, what?

He was nineteen—old enough, by the Lord Harry—and even if the Gruber girl was fifteen years his senior, a bit of mature cracklin' might do the idiot some good. Apart from anything else, the money meant luxuries such as food and shoes . . . Sir Henry's mouth watered as he thought of a gobbet of sirloin.

He turned to his wife and cleared his throat. 'Julia, old thing,' he barked, 'I have given my consent for Mrs Gruber's daughter to marry Peregrine. It's a purely business arrangement—in return for Peregrine's hand for the gel, Mrs Gruber will see to it that our financial problems are solved. The future of Hawsbortem Towers will be secure. What d'you say to that, my dear?'

Lady Julia did not answer.

Sir Henry grew purple and spat: 'Confound it, woman, will you listen to me? God's blood, we need the money! Damn it, the boy must pop back into the world sometime, don't you know! He can't stay marooned in the blasted library for ever—it's time he warmed his tripes.'

In reply to the tirade Lady Julia rose to her full height, and began to float out of the room. 'Henry,' she said in a low controlled voice, 'I shall not keep your company until you can compose yourself. Your language is that of a costermonger. Kindly ring for Albert to perambulate my afternoon tea and Bath Olivers into the armoury.'

She drifted from the room, rather like a bank of fog. Sir Henry's bucolic features creased with utter despair, and he slumped into the chair so recently vacated by his wife and started to chew her needlework.

I read this peculiar missive, then forgot about it. But a few days later I received another letter from the doughty Miss Pluckett.

March 23rd

Dear Mr Dawson,

I thought I would have heard from you, but it's quite apparent you thought the MS was an exercise in banality. I assure you I didn't make it up.

Since my last correspondence with you, a further document has come into my hands. It fell from Sir Peregrine's pocket whilst he was standing on his head during a yoga class run by an accordianist.

This document gives the story a different point of view.

So, enclosed please find the Peregrine Oswald Potts-Belching memoirs. He won't mind—he'd only have chewed it with his whinberry yogurt.

Yours ever,

Amy Pluckett (miss)

Amy Pluckett (Miss)

ps Was Errol Flynn a bit that way?

The Mansion
Lytham St Anne's
March 25th

Dear Miss Pluckett,

When I'd finally succeeded in deciphering the meandering scrawl that lay submerged in a layer of chip fat, I found it a deeply moving tale unlike anything I'd ever perused before.

If you catch that poor man on his head again, do filch some more of his writing before he digests them with a sweetmeat.

Yours,

Les Dawson

Les Dawson (Mr)

ps I never knew Mr Errol Flynn, but I am informed that his reputation precludes him from any suggestion of sodomy.

WHEN MY papa loftily informed me that I was to be wed without delay to the awesome Mrs Gruber's dough-faced daughter, my first impulse was to leap like a startled fawn into a cupboard and have a private drama. Unashamedly, I burst into a positive cataract of tears. You will doubtless appreciate my blind panic when I tell you that—despite my nineteen summers—I had never had a jot to do with females. My knowledge of the opposite sex was limited to mama, dear nanny, and the occasional glimpses I'd had of the dreadful Gruber women, stalking about the place as if on safari.

No, dear reader, I had no experience with what novelists coyly refer to as 'the gentle sex'. And Mrs Gruber's daughter Greta looked anything but gentle. In fact on one occasion, whilst playing my harp, I chanced to look out of the window, and I saw the oafish lady pole-axe a cow with an uppercut!

My world was the cloistered Valhalla of the library, the beauty that my dear late and lamented tutor, Trevor, introduced me to. I never, ever wanted to leave my world, my lovely celibate realm of books and poetry, my beloved harp and flutes. The universe beyond the library is too corybantic for a person as deeply sensitive as I.

On the odd occasion that I girded my loins with courage, and ventured forth on a tentative exploration of the rest of the house, my mama completely ignored me. Indeed, on one of my cautious forays, she mistook me for an intruder and had me thrashed by a rented ghillie. Reality for me was a sonnet by Will the Bard; a chapter from Balzac . . . I could plummet into an abyss of sadness over the agony endured by Latude, I drooled in euphoria when sweet Bach stirred my soul with a cadenza and soared like an egret with a minim by Wagner . . .

I am alone! Dear Trevor, gone forever and all through the rancid jaws of an elderly mastiff! No more will his beautiful fingers run through my fair locks; no more will he croon the lyrics of Yeats, or retell the epic of Hero and Leander. No more will he hold me in his tender embrace as we watch the waxen moon ride across the heavens, like unto a yellow chariot, towards the ebon blackness of the infinite, wherein the tethered bulks of Jupiter and Mars hang festooned for all time in their orbital majesty.

Following my papa's dictum, all manner of creatures commenced an invasion of my domain. Firstly, Albert the footman—acting on orders—stripped my of my velvet pantaloons and flounced blouse, and dressed me in some awful fustian, purchased from a company of clothiers known as 'Burton's'. My silken drawers were removed forcibly and in their stead, I had to don cotton briefs that chafed my delicate nether limbs. Worse was to come: the village barber arrived and he took great delight in shearing off my shoulder-length blond curls, the curls that dear Trevor had so often fondled. My harp was thrown into the empty West Wing and no longer was I to be allowed to perform my solo minuet by moonlight . . . Horror upon horror, heaped on my luckless shoulders. Oh Trevor, why should a horse, a dog, a rat have life . . . and thou no breath at all?

A week later, like a well-scrubbed scarifice, I was formally introduced to my prospective bride, and I nearly dissolved at the sight of the ageing jade. Much older than I of course, built like a brick out-house, with a face like a tin of condemned veal, her eyes were chilled flints that pierced my very marrow. Her teeth, what was left of them, reminded me of a well-worn harpsichord keyboard, and her lips were vast blubbery tubes; when she lightly kissed me upon my cheek, it felt as though I had been savaged by a frankfurter. I recoiled in stark terror when her mother, Mrs Gruber, embraced me with the sort of grip one expects from a mechanical shovel. This woman repelled me even more: her eyes burned, pits of raging coals, her mouth was a thin slit with slivers of spittle moistening the membranes in spools . . . and she needed a shave.

Papa tried to jolly up the proceedings by sending Albert to the cellars, to rummage for the odd bottle of port, and dear mama asked me twice who I was. The wine loosened the tongues of the absurd gathering and Mrs Gruber commanded the company to drink to somebody called 'Mein Hermann'. I pleaded that I had a headache and, after my bride-to-be had fondled my buttocks and I had endured Mrs Gruber's comments about my lack of masculinity, I fled in a cloud of

tears to my room. I flung myself on the pillows, and wept for
Trevor.

That, my dearest reader, was my ghastly engagement
party, the portals to a nightmare that was to take me to the
very rim of madness.

The Institution,
Miresea-on-Crouch
April 4th

Dear Mr Dawson,
Isn't it a lovely day? The gardens here are so very beautiful, and lots of
people are playing leapfrog.
Now, Mr Dawson, the next events seem to have been remembered ever
so clearly—but then they do say that everyone loves a wedding. Do you
still recall yours?
Yours ever,

Amy Pluckett (Miss)

Amy Pluckett (Miss)

The Mansion,
Lytham St Anne's
April 5th

Dear Miss Pluckett,
The memory of my wedding day is etched firmly in my mind—but they
do say time is a great healer.
Yours bitterly,

Les Dawson

Les Dawson

PEREGRINE OSWALD Potts-Belching was married to Greta Gruber on the tenth of June, 1948, and Ruff-on-the-Ole will never forget it—even though time is a great healer.

Everything augured well at first: the sun bled its rays over the tiny village church, and the shafts of warmth shone through the vandalised stained glass windows and mellowed the gnarled Saxon stones. Sir Henry and Lady Julia sat in the family pew, and behind them, the remnants of the Potts-Belching clan. There was old Griswald Potts-Belching who was quite mad and already asleep; one Sudbury Fanshawe-Getty, who had married Sir Henry's eldest sister, Miriam—he had lost an arm at Jutland and his foot in a faulty stirrup. He was a tall man who drank like a demented carp and couldn't pee. Miriam, his wife, bred turtles and took orphans to Bognor. Lady Julia's brother Caspar lolled on his seat, reading a copy of *The Nudist Review*, he hadn't worked since before the war and was wanted by a detective in Casablanca. And last—but never least—sat Sir Henry's cousin, Emily Hattersley-Crowe, a maiden lady who claimed she had been raped by a man from Pluto. Across from the Potts-Belchings, sat the Grubers: Mrs Gruber, the two square men who had tossed Henry into the horse trough, and immediately behind them four rows of pews jammed with hard blond men with duelling scars and a row of dough-faced women—all pregnant. The villagers stood at the rear of the church, stunned.

The organist, Mr Moon, struck up with the doom-laden theme of 'The Wedding March' and the straggle of choir boys rose to their feet. The Very Reverend Horace Mycroft could barely suppress a shudder as he gazed at the Gruber horde, and he threw a sympathetic glance at the young, whey-faced bridegroom who stood trembling at his father's side. Even from where he stood, the Reverend Mycroft could plainly see that Albert had the bridegroom's arm twisted behind his back.

A gasp of fright came from the open-mouthed villagers as the bride entered the church. Dressed in white, she looked like a beached whale as she began her march down the aisle. Her two bridesmaids (it was said later) wore gun holsters on the hip as they convoyed the bride to the altar. Peregrine was seen to look furtively over his shoulder and, when he espied his advancing fate, something snapped in the lad. He broke away from Albert, and vaulted over the altar rail shouting at the top of his voice: 'Sanctuary!' Peregrine never made his escape for one of the square men leaped forward and felled the fleeing youth with an incense burner, dropping the luckless bridegroom into a heap at the vestry door.

Uproar ensued, but was swiftly hushed by Mrs Gruber who shoved the Reverend Mycroft out of the way, firing a Luger into the air as she did so. Villagers who tried to leave the church were hurled back by the large blond young men, working as a team. Sir Henry and his family watched the events aghast, but nobody went to Peregrine's aid as the two square men frogmarched him back to the altar, where he was joined by the bride-to-be. She tucked the bridegroom under her arm and urged the vicar to get on with the wedding; in a daze, the Reverend Mycroft complied and the terrible ceremony went ahead.

After it was all over, Mrs Gruber scattered money to the villagers and, in the mad scramble that followed, Peregrine and his bride were ushered away from the church, and back to Hawsbortem Towers. The scene which followed gave Sir Henry the willies. Caterers had decked the gloomy dining salon into something resembling gaiety, and a long trestle table groaning with food had been placed down the centre of the stone-flagged chamber. The blond young men herded all the other guests into a line and thrust a glass and a plate into their hands without so much as a 'by your leave'.

Despite their grave misgivings about the whole deeply-suspect nuptuals, the sheer weight of food and drink soon nullified the doubts expressed by the guests, and even a little jollity began to creep into the celebration. Mrs Gruber's speech, which was full of condemnation for the Poles, didn't shock as one might have expected. Sir Henry's long-winded oratory was stilled by a well-aimed bath bun, and Lady Julia inquired if Mr Baldwin was still Prime Minister.

It was observed, however, that Peregrine was the colour of oiled marble, and was seen from time to time to fan himself with a small sachet of pure lavender. His bride, by contrast, straddled the table and drank straight from the bottle, shouting filthy slogans, until Mrs Gruber smacked her head with the silver cruet. Finally, Greta yanked her unwilling husband to his dainty feet and dragged him off to the bridal chamber.

It is said in the village that Peregrine's screams could be plainly heard as far as the old turnpike, and Crafty George, the local poacher, swore on oath, that he had seen a naked Peregrine being chased around the moat by his bride waving a cutlass.

A pall of silence fell on the old grey house as the months passed, and even Albert stopped his weekly jaunt to the Frog and Elk. Tourists who asked the locals about Hawsbortem Towers were given short shrift and sent on their way from Ruff-on-the-Ole with nothing but trinkets depicting the times when Roundheads watered their steeds at Clogg's Well.

Rumour of course refused to die. There were tales of brass bands playing, of marching feet echoing at midnight, of rifle fire coming from the woods; but it was mere speculation, and nobody took it seriously until Crafty George vanished in early September 1954.

The Institution,
Miresea-on-Crouch
April 13th

Dear Mr Dawson,

In my desire to get to the bottom of this story, I have taken to following Sir Peregrine further afield. Last night I watched him playing his flute to a bullock and, as he pranced—dressed in his caftan with the handkerchief hem—I took the liberty of extracting lots of papers from the elasticated knickers of his regulation underdrawers.

These vital documents sent my senses reeling with excitement.

Yours ever,

Amy Pluckett (Miss)

Amy Pluckett (Miss)

ps I was never sure of James Robertson Justice, were you?

SIR ALDRED Wainwright-Baggshot, head of the British Secret
Service in September 1954, didn't look like a James Bond. In
features he rather favoured a bilious canary, and when he
was worried—as indeed on that blustery day in March, he
was—his eyes tended to cross so much that among the
myriads of civil servants who saturated his office block in
Whitehall he was known as England's answer to Ben Turpin.

He had just replaced the telephone after receiving a
blistering call from the P.M. about several incidents that had
occurred early that year. There had been a small riot in the
East End of London, and the authorities believed that a
faction of neo-Nazis had been involved. In Bonn, an ex-S.S.
officer had been towed away to Israel on war crime charges;
he had stated, in his cups, that his beloved Leader had not
died in the Berlin bunker, but had escaped and would soon
rise again and knock the balls off the British and the
Americans.

Down in rural Dorset, a poacher had vanished from the
face of the earth, and his wife demanded his return, or
substantial compensation. The most pressing matter,
however, was the theft of three tanks from Bovington.
Wainwright-Baggshot sighed wearily and broke wind. The
telephone rang again and, after listening carefully,
Wainwright-Baggshot wrote on his notepad, 'Get sliced loaf
and jar of glazed cherries.' He slammed the receiver back on

to its cradle, and wished his wife would do her own shopping.

A knock on the door made him sit upright and clear his throat. He commanded the knocker to enter, and he set his lips in a thin hard line that made him look like a slashed melon. A tall man glided into the room, a tall, spare well-dressed man, whose name was Rodney Barton, double O in the section, licensed to kill and eligible for a staff pension at fifty-five.

'Well, Barton, what you have got for me? The P.M. hauled me over the coals not ten minutes ago. I must tell him that there's some progress, otherwise I'll never get to Brighton for the weekend.' Having delivered that short diatribe, Wainwright-Baggshot lit his pipe and burned his thumb on the match.

Barton watched his chief howling with pain, and leaping up and down, with barely concealed contempt. He knew that Wainwright-Baggshot was an idiot, for whom the post of caretaker would have taxed his limited intellectual resources. But for Rodney, Wainwright-Baggshot's imbecility was an asset; he would believe most awful whoppers. Despite his double O Barton had never killed anybody; and his record as a sharp, swashbuckling agent was entirely developed from his fertile imagination, and put down in print by a nubile clerk in the archives who adored Barton, and believed every word he told her. If any danger threatened British security abroad or on home ground, Rodney sent his Aunt Maude to deal with it.

Rodney had first stumbled on her potential while observing her strangle his uncle after a tiff concerning rissoles for supper. So adroit was his aunt in dispatching her mate that her nephew helped her dissolve the body in a bath of acid and spend uncle's Post Office savings. In a three-year period, Aunt Maude had butchered two Rumanians, a Turk, and a Russian pervert, and that was a pretty good track record for a frail eighty-year-old, well-bred lady. As a reward, Barton would take her down into a cellar in Bond Street, and let her run riot with prisoners of the State until they talked—which they did after ten minutes with her. Thus, Rodney had time to pursue his real interests (riding every available female in sight and, as he looked quite a lot like Clark Gable, the supply was endless).

But this business of the tank thefts was a little worrying; and Rodney realised that because of the pressure being brought to bear on old Wainwright-Baggshot, he would have to pull the proverbial digit out and do a spot of snooping, taking Auntie along in case of peril to life and limb.

Barton waited until his chief had ceased wagging his scorched thumb about, then spoke rapidly to him. 'From what we have gleaned, sir, it would seem that the tanks were stolen during the night of the twenty-fourth—the sentries on duty were doped by something put into their urn of tea. Frankly though, what I remember of Army tea, it didn't need anything added to put one out what? Hahaha.'

Wainwright-Baggshot shuddered and gave Rodney a wintery grimace. 'This is not the Chiswick Empire, Barton,' he intoned. 'Keep what passes for a sense of humour out of it. Damn it, man, someone pinches three tanks, the latest Centurions with stabilisers, from under our very smellers! It is deplorable, and somebody's head will roll for it. Now again, what have you for me?'

Rodney grew his grave face and, standing stiffly, began to recite: 'The tank tracks were followed to the edge of a small village, not far from Corfe Castle, but then had been obliterated. The name of the village is Ruff-on-the-Ole, and we have a team down there now making intensive inquiries. We think there is a link-up between the theft of the tanks and the total disappearance of a local poacher known as Crafty George.'

'Do you think this poacher chap is tied up with the missing tanks?' said Wainwright-Baggshot testily.

Rodney shook his head. 'No link at present, sir, but my men are working on it. Another odd thing's popped up, it seems that the trouble in the East End was engineered by a man who lives near Ruff-on-the-Ole. We don't know who the man is, but one of our agents got into conversation with the landlord of the local pub, the Frog and Elk—apparently they do an absolutely super ploughman's lunch, and the ale is . . .'

Wainwright-Baggshot went puce and thundered, 'Confound it, Barton, stick to the point. Really, this is bloody serious.'

Rodney, realising that he had gone over the top, became solemn as an owl and resumed. 'Sorry sir. Well, the landlord told our man that there were several strangers who came into the pub from time to time and, although he couldn't be sure, he got the impression they were Germans.'

Wainwright-Baggshot's mouth dropped open like a cash register. 'Krauts? In Dorset? Can't be tourists surely. I mean, well, they've been beaten.'

Dutifully, Rodney nodded his head. 'I wouldn't have thought so, sir, the Jerries can't be prosperous enough for holidays yet, but there is another strange thing that came out in conversation. It seems that four miles from the village is a sort of stately old pile known as Hawsbortem Towers, the home of the Potts-Belching family. Now here *is* a curious thing: in 1948, the son, one Peregrine Oswald, was married to the daughter of an old German woman who cleaned at the Towers. In those days, the staff at the Towers consisted of three people, plus Sir Henry and Lady Potts-Belching and their son Peregrine. Total? Six people. Apparently now the staff is rumoured to muster about a hundred and fifty, if the provisions drawn from the local store are anything to go by.'

Wainwright-Baggshot sat back stunned. 'Good grief, what the hell is going on down there? Now look here, Barton, you'd better be off to that infernal village, and be quick about it. I don't like any of this, and I'm damned if I'm going to miss my weekend at Brighton.'

With that, the chief dismissed Rodney with a wave of his hand, and picked up the telephone.

The Institution,
Miresea-on-Crouch
April 18th

Dear Les,

I do hope you don't mind if I call you that. 'Mr Dawson' seems so cold and formal when we are sharing this emotional experience.

My heart bleeds for Peregrine Oswald! How anyone could treat a being so sensitive so cruelly . . .

Read for yourself.

Yours, deeply moved,

Amy Pluckett (Miss)

Amy Pluckett (Miss)

The Mansion,
Lytham St Anne's
April 20th

Dear Miss Pluckett,

I think I'd be happier if you were moved even further.

Yours etc.,

Les Dawson

Les Dawson

But I read on . . .

Sir Peregrine Oswald Potts-Belching's memoir

SIX YEARS have elapsed since papa sold me—lock, stock and body—to Greta Gruber; a bondage more horrifying than anything dreamed up by a drink-maddened Poe. Since that first night when she threw me naked on to the bed then—realising that I made poor fodder for her impassioned appetite—chased me around the perimeter of the moat, she has beaten me like a gong, humiliated me, and kept me a veritable prisoner in the bedroom. Fortunately, I know of a secret passage which opens behind the commode on the landing; and when she is in her cups—which is frequently—I steal away down the musty tunnel, and find solace with my flute.

Six years of pure Hell, and I know only too well that I will never be permitted to escape—I know far too much about what is afoot in Hawsbortem Towers. It started soon after our marriage. After the initial onslaught on my body she soon tired of hitting me, and I discovered that she was taking many lovers. To my intense chagrin, one of the men she bedded was papa.

One rather gloomy Sunday evening, I was creeping round the house via my secret passage and found myself peering through a hole just above a portrait of Isaac Potts-Belching, the club-footed second baronet who lost his ear in a circular saw. Through the hole I squinted, and suddenly into view came Frau Gruber with six of her big blond relations. But caressing Frau Gruber was—Greta!

I had of course read about the goings-on in the Isle of Lesbos . . . you know, where ladies sort of did things with ladies. Not that I'm a prude about that way of behaving; well, I mean, Trevor had initiated me into what he called 'the Greek love'. Oh, Trevor! But really, mother and daughter?

My musings were interrupted when Frau Gruber took off her grey hair . . . Oh Lord, I thought, she's bald. But no—under the wig the grisly parent had black hair, the forelock of which hung down over her left eye . . . They kissed and roared with laughter, and both of them embraced a stockily-built man who had just entered the room. A sinister type who rarely spoke, I'd first noticed him at our wedding; Greta called him 'Martin'.

They all seemed in high spirits, and talked animatedly in German. Some of the beefy blond men started to sing a song that reminded me of marching; one in particular had a good voice, nice-looking he was . . . I was getting hot under the collar, and missing Trevor, so I crept away back to my room.

Another night, I distinctly heard the sound of people moving about in the shrubbery. I dressed, tiptoed down the passage and found an exit from the east side of the house; it opened on a mass of weeds in a disused drain and from there I watched the blond men doing some exercise with guns. There seemed to be more and more of them, some shouting orders and others crashing through the shrubbery. When one came close to me I retraced my steps back into the passage, post haste.

Within only a year of our ill-fated nuptials, it became obvious that something was going on at the Towers. My mother, Lady Julia, was moved into the West Turret by Frau Gruber's troop; she didn't seem to mind at all, and they treated her with great respect throughout the transfer. Papa spent all his time guzzling port, and Frau Gruber kept him in a state of euphoria with ample cash and brawny maidens imported from Ruff-on-the-Ole. In the next five years the Grubers took over more and more of the running of Hawsbortem Towers, and from the garbled conversations I overheard it seemed that the village was also in their leathery grasp.

One afternoon, after Greta had staggered into my bedroom and beaten me with a broom-handle, I decided I would have to attempt flight from my ludicrous situation. As soon as my drink-sodden wife fell into a stupor, I crept out of the room and into the secret passage—determined to find an egress for my escape. Muttered voices from the armoury halted my intention—gingerly, I slid back a wooden disc which I knew covered a tiny hole in the belly-button of Mars in a mural on the other side of the wall. I could see the bewigged Frau Gruber, talking to a man whose face was vaguely familiar . . . It belonged to a prominent trade union leader, who had recently terrified the country with the threat of a miners' strike. I could hear only snatches of their conversation, and it made no sense at all:

Gruber: 'Then you agree? Best for everybody . . . I give you my word . . .' (I strained to hear the mumbling, and a sliver of dowel went up my nose.)

Trade Unionist: 'Behind you all the way . . . Vote my way . . . Sure of E.T.U. . . . Take over stations . . .'

Gruber: 'Make a move soon . . . Money coming . . . make contacts . . .'

The man shook Gruber's hand, and left the armoury.

Before I could digest what I had overheard, a sudden moan jolted me—it seemed to come from lower down the passage. My heart lurched when it happened again, and this time it was accompanied by the sound of a whiplash. Trembling like an aspen, I softly made my way to where the noise had been emitted. There was no further sound, and I would have left it alone if I hadn't heard a door being bolted—then I knew where the moan had come from.

The butler's pantry was a small dank chamber, long disused, and I had to worm my way toward the wall that formed the rear of it, for bricks and wooden beams had blocked the narrow corridor. At last I reached the wall—as far as I could see, there was no peephole. But the mortar between the flaking stones had crumbled to dust, so it was a matter of finding something to scrape a hole through a joint in the wall. A long rusty nail did the trick, and soon I was peering through the cavity. What I saw caused me to feel quite faint.

Strung up, with ropes around his wrists, was Crafty George, the poacher. He was naked from the waist up, and although the chamber was gloomy—lit by only a single small light bulb—I could see the marks of a whip across his shoulders. His head was thrown back, and he was moaning like a stricken animal—the hairs on my neck stiffened.

I bolted rabbit-fashion, back up the passage, whimpering as I stumbled along to where it broadened. In my desire to get away from the horror of Crafty George's incarceration, I took a different route from the one that would have led me back to the panelling behind the commode on the landing, and I found myself in a very unfamiliar part of the labyrinth.

I paused for breath, trying to regain my bearings; it wasn't going to be easy. Hawsbortem Towers was riddled with passages and hidey-holes; rumour had it that two detachments of Prince Rupert's mercenaries had been hidden from Cromwell's men for over three months; and even before the Civil War eighty persecuted monks had found refuge in a secret room behind the wine bins. Only the fact that they had imbibed too freely led to their capture by their pursuers, who heard them singing monastery favourites.

Nobody knows who had originally built the Towers, but the house dated back to the time of the Crusades, and had been used—so Ruff-on-the-Ole legend had it—'For the lads to have a bit of a do afore going off to give Saladin a good hiding.' In happier times, Trevor and I had pored over old books, looking for a clue as to the builder's identity—but all that emerged from our study was that the Towers had been up for a long time before being granted to the Potts-Belchings for 'services rendered to the Crown'.

Now I was lost, and aching to go to the lavatory. I crept along the strange route, and found myself in a large chamber which was empty—apart from a skeleton chained to the wall. I turned about and sped away, on and on through the narrow passage—then stopped in my tracks at the sound of engines being revved harshly.

Breathless, I crouched down by the wall, and carefully removed a piece of wood hinged to the stone face of the buttress. An aperture swung into my vision and in the vast stone-lined vault it revealed (I assumed it was part of the cellar complex), I saw three huge tanks being positioned by Gruber's blond men—who were all wearing battle-dress.

By this time, my senses were in a turmoil, and I found it all too much to comprehend—but one thing I knew with clarity: I had to get away and tell somebody about what was going on at the Towers.

I still cannot recall how I discovered the correct route that took me back to the commode. But I did, and crept back to the bedroom. I sank on to my bed with a heart beating like a kettle-drum. I must have dropped off into a fitful slumber, because I was awakened by Greta, who brought me back to the surface of consciousness by the simple expedient of slapping me about the face with her grimy paw.

'Where have you been?' she yelled into my ear.

'Oh, I just went for a stroll,' I managed to vouchsafe.

'From now on, my little wanderer, you will stay in your room. Is that clear?' she stormed at me.

I nodded dumbly. Greta frightened me to my very roots, and physically—as I knew from past experiences—she was more than capable of turning me into a pain-laden mass of offal. To emphasise her warning, she picked me up and tossed me against a wardrobe, then trundled out of the room. I heard her lock the door behind her.

It was apparent even to someone like myself that something was brewing, and I didn't think it boded well for Papa and Mama—or me. I had to get out. Frantically, I walked up and down trying to think of some method of opening the bedroom door, which—being solid oak —presented quite a problem. In a fit of impotent rage I banged my fist against the wooden panelling lining the room, and with a protesting groan a section yawned open. Yet another hidden facet of the house was revealed. Inside the passage I could see nothing of any interest, except a rusty sabre and a pike which I decided to take along with me as a means of defence.

This tunnel, I realised, must run at the back of Greta's bedroom; and, having ascertained that the gorgon wasn't in there, I decided to find a way in—the germ of an idea had kindled in my fevered imagination. It took only a moment to discover that by pressing hard on a wooden slat, part of the wall would open up—I was in Greta's odious quarters!

Swiftly, I rummaged through her wardrobe and selected a dress which looked as if it might fit me. I also purloined a blond wig I hadn't seen her wear recently. My idea was that I would stand a better chance of making my escape from the Towers, by now a fortress, if I was disguised as a girl. The Gruber louts, who were liberally sprinkled about the estate, might mistake me for one of those imported from Ruff-on-the-Ole as bed companions for them and Papa.

Curiosity made me linger a while and peep into the drawers of Greta's dressing-table—there was the usual feminine trivia, plus two Luger pistols and a belt of ammunition. I was about to take my leave when I noticed a large photograph of Greta, with a background of snow-capped mountains behind her. Something was written at the bottom of the snap, a trifle faded with time; but one thing did stand out—the name 'Eva'. I hastily put the photograph back and, making a bundle of the dress and wig and a pair of high-heeled shoes, I withdrew from the room and got back into my passage, I resealed the panel, then stripped myself naked—leaving on only my cotton drawers—donned the dress and shoes, panting with anxiety as I did so, and finally jammed the wig on my head. As an afterthought I re-entered Greta's room and surveyed myself in the mirror to make sure I didn't look like something out of a Ben Travers farce. Frankly, I looked very pretty—and I blushed as I imagined what dear Trevor would have said.

Closing the panel behind me again, I lofted the pike on to my shoulder and commenced to creep down the stifling passage. I had gone only a few yards when I heard Crafty George moaning again . . .

Despite my desire to escape, I couldn't leave the poor wretch to yet further torment; so I made my way to the wall of the butler's pantry and, cautiously, started to break some of it down. I made a hole just big enough, and struggled through it.

Crafty George was half unconscious and didn't notice me. I immediately put the bricks back to hide the hole I had made and, as an added precaution, I pulled an old wine rack across as well. It was very dark in that corner, and the chance of anybody prying there was remote, but I couldn't afford the discovery of my secret passage.

I was about to undo the bonds holding Crafty George when I heard a bolt being drawn back—I nearly screamed with fright, and scrabbled for cover under a table. One of the blond giants entered the pantry, closely examined Crafty George, slapped him on the face; when there was no response from the hapless rustic, he marched out banging the door behind him, but not bolting it.

I waited a few moments, then recommenced sawing the ropes with the edge of the pike. It seemed to take an age before Crafty George fell to the floor unfettered, and I had to sit down and try to control my trembling limbs. I bent over the poacher, who was still moaning softly, and I hadn't a clue what to do to revive him. I really did feel most inept, and was about to run hither and thither like a cockerel without a head, when I spotted a bucket of water under the table. I picked it up, and threw the contents over Crafty George.

It certainly did the trick; the old rogue coughed and

spluttered, shook his rangy head and opened his eyes—I saw fear followed by puzzlement when he saw me.

'Who the hell are you, miss?' he whispered. 'Are you one of them or summat? I tell thee, I know nowt!'

I put my face close to his. 'Don't you recognise me? I'm Peregrine Oswald Potts-Belching.'

He looked at me and my attire, open-mouthed. 'So tha's finally gone over the top, have yer?' he said.

I ignored the salty remark, and replied spiritedly, 'I have just cut you down, my good man. At least you could show some gratitude! And I might add that I'm dressed like this hoping to escape from the Towers—I know something's going on. Tell me all *you* know.'

He nodded. 'Sorry, master, and I thank you. All as I know is I were in the woods looking for the odd rabbit or two, when I saw them big fellers tramping through the trees with rifles. One of 'em saw me, an' next thing I knew, I'd been belted on the head and I woke up in here. They gave me the lash, and started asking me all sorts of questions—I told 'em I knew nowt, but they kept bashin' me.'

'We've got to get out of here, George,' I said lamely. 'Can you walk all right? This part of the house is fairly unused; with luck we can get into the grounds through the old servants' quarters.'

George shook his head. 'Nay, young master, we'll not do it. What you need to get away is a diversion. You're young, you have a chance.' He stopped, deep in thought. 'If we can get to the grounds,' he said, 'I'll create a bit of a noise and draw them away from you. Then you make a bolt for it.'

I was stunned by his bravery. 'But they'll catch you again and do the most awful things to you,' I said to him urgently.

Crafty George smiled thinly. 'I fought the buggers in the First World War, lad, and I owe the swine for a couple of mates who didn't come back.' So saying, he gestured to me to assist him to his feet; it was obvious that he was very weak.

We listened at the door for a moment, but all was quiet. I opened the door, its rusty hinges squealing a protest, and George and I inched our way through into the corridor beyond.

The butler's pantry was situated in a part of the Towers

which had been closed off for many years, and it smelt like it. High grime-encrusted windows defied the sun's rays to fret their way in, the stone-flagged floors had a coating of dust so thick in parts that it rose in wreaths as our footsteps sank into it. There was no sign of any activity anywhere, and my confidence rose . . .

I was brought back to reality when Crafty George violently tugged my arm, and dragged me behind a large chipped bust of Voltaire. He gestured to me to be quiet, and I soon saw why—only a few feet away sat a burly Gruber cohort. His back was towards us, and his head was slowly going up and down. I was wondering why, until George whispered, 'He's asleep!'

We crept forward; the blond thug was indeed in the arms of the Sandman. We sidled past, Crafty George pausing to pick up a most revolting-looking firearm that was propped near the slumbering menace. Any minute, I expected to hear a shout, but the gods were on our side for the moment; and Crafty George and I were soon outside a heavily-carved door which I felt should lead through into the vegetable garden.

The door took an age to open but, finally, the old poacher had managed to prise open a space twixt door and wall wide enough for us to wriggle through and creep out into the overgrown wilderness that had once housed vast tiers of baleful broccoli.

In his desire to flee the scene of his imprisonment, Crafty George shot off towards the garden wall which escorted a narrow lane leading to Ruff-on-the-Ole. In one marathon effort he bounded over it like a kangaroo that's just had a promise—and left me quaking, to panic.

I commenced to tiptoe through the tall weeds; they tugged at my dress and impeded my progress. I was so preoccupied in rescuing myself from nettles and the like that I failed to notice I was heading straight for Frau Gruber. Too late, I found myself face to face with her, and she threw her arms around me in a grip that would have bent a girder.

I closed my eyes, waiting for the roar of recognition, but none was forthcoming. Instead, when I risked opening my eyes, it was to find Frau Gruber looking at me with a glance of admiration, and breathing heavily.

'Where are you going, my lovely?' the awful apparition said softly.

'I'm trying to find my way out, back to the village, madam,' I replied, hoping that Frau Gruber would mistake me for one of the village girls who kept the imported blond army happy.

'Well, *mein leibling*, there is no hurry . . . Come, give me a kiss,' Gruber hissed.

Suddenly, it dawned on me—the old ratbag fancied me! Oh God, I thought, I'd need a tin opener to get out of this.

'Please, madam, you mustn't,' I panted. 'You are a lady. I mean . . . well, I'm not a girl like that.'

Frau Gruber in response threw off her wig and ripped her blouse apart to reveal a chest so hairy it looked like a burst sofa. 'Let this be our secret. I'm a man—a very lonely man!' With that, I was kissed soundly on the cheek with lips that were like an inner tube.

We struggled and threshed about as he tried to take my frock off; finally, I resorted to a flood of tears. Instantly, Gruber was contrite.

'Oh, I make you unhappy, yes?'

I nodded and whispered, 'I've never done anything like this before . . . please, be kind.' It did the trick.

Gruber motioned that we should sit down on a sack of decayed fertiliser and, with his arm draped around my shoulders, he told me that from now on I was to be his lady friend, *ja*? That he wouldn't press his desire on me until I was ready and, from now on, I would have a room next to his—but not to tell anyone of our relationship. Especially not his daughter, Greta.

It was fine by me. I had a breathing space in which to plan another escape and I'd be rid of his rotten daughter. I nodded in agreement, and promised to keep away from everyone else. He beamed and embraced me yet again, hoisted me to my feet and together we sidled off to his suite of rooms, avoiding contact with the square blond men who swarmed about the place.

What I didn't know was that Crafty George, having got safely away, had had a twinge of conscience—perhaps remembering his promise to create a diversion so that *I* could

escape—and had returned to see what had happened to me.
From his vantage point atop the wall, he had seen 'Frau'
Gruber making up to me with passion . . .

The Institution,
Miresea-on-Crouch
April 27th

Dearest Leslie,
I did not wish to be so familiar, but I feel a rapport with you. Perhaps a
man of the world like yourself can have little idea of how provocative this
tale is to someone who has led my sort of secluded life. But I took your
advice and moved further away in my watch on Sir Peregrine.
Now I'm in a thicket quite near a clearing where Peregrine paints his
vest and quotes sonnets from the great bard.
Must go—my cardi is caught on a bramble.
Yours ever,

Amy Pluckett (Miss)

Amy Pluckett (Miss)

The Mansion,
Lytham St Anne's
April 30th

Dear Miss Pluckett,
First underdrawers, now a vest! My dear lady, this a veritable windfall
to the *News of the World*.
Yours,

Les Dawson

Les Dawson

THERE WERE four men in Sir Aldred Wainwright-Baggshot's office, and he wasn't one of them. The head of the British Secret Service was in Brighton playing bridge with his cronies, losing a fair bit of money, but looking forward to an evening with a Miss Goldie Balhou, a well-respected stripper from Shepherd's Bush. The four men consisted of Sam Kantor, a prominent CIA agent; the Prime Minister; Ivan Karpov, the Russian Under-Secretary; and, recently recalled from Dorset, Rodney Barton.

It was Sam Kantor who broke the oppressive silence first. 'We have always suspected that Adolf Hitler and Eva Braun escaped from the bunker. The suicide was too pat, too well-engineered, and ever since then, Mr Prime Minister, we have worked alongside our Russian allies in an effort to find them. Until 1947, the trail was cold; then we had a stroke of luck. A British soldier who stayed on in Holland after the war told one of our men that a certain Army Captain of Dragoons, Sir Henry Potts-Belching, had smuggled back to England two women. The soldier himself had driven the captain and the women to the coast. The soldier was no fool and he informed our man that, in his opinion, the elder of the two women was, in fact, a man.' The other three men hung on every word spoken by Sam Kantor, then the Russian, lighting up a black cigarette, enlarged on the data already expounded by the American.

'There was a break-out in a prisoner-of-war camp in the Ukraine in 1946, many Russian soldiers were killed in the uprising and, regrettably, over two hundred Nazi fanatics escaped. Some were captured and died amid shouts of: "He lives . . . The Fuhrer lives." We now know that over fifty of these fanatics managed to get to England . . . Yes, my dear Prime Minister, to your country. Since 1946, in Britain there have been many strikes, most of which you think are caused by—what is the term? Oh yes, left-wing radicals. Nothing could be further from the truth, my friend, the fact is this: the leader of the so called trade union movement is, in fact, a German, Hans Sneezle, a most dedicated Nazi. In every branch of trade unionism, there is to be found such a man.'

The British Prime Miniser sat back stunned, and decided to throw in the towel at the next election. Sam Kantor nodded in brooding agreement with his Russian ally, and resumed.

'We had no idea where Hitler was holed up, until a guy from Dorset—a poacher I think you call this type of crook—was brought here by your Mr Barton, and what he told us makes it clear that Adolf Hitler and Eva Braun are living in a place called Hawsbortem Towers, the ancestral home of the Potts-Belching family, and our Captain Sir Henry is the present owner of the place. It is a veritable fortress, with something like three hundred armed men on the premises, and that's not all . . . The three stolen tanks are there in the grounds of Hawsbortem Towers.'

The Prime Minister paled visibly and sank lower in his seat.

Sam Kantor went on: 'It's a screwy arrangement—in return for keeping the old house up to scratch, Hitler got Eva to marry Henry's only son, Peregrine Oswald. And here's the ludicrous part of it all . . . Henry's son is a fag.'

The Prime Minister shot upright and blurted out: 'What? Are you trying to tell me that this Peregrine feller is a pouffe? A bloody fruit?'

Kantor smiled thinly. 'Yes, apparently he's as bent as a nine-dollar note.'

The Prime Minister picked his chin up from the floor and put it between his shaking hands. 'What are we waiting for? For God's sake, let's get in and shift the buggers out.'

The Russian, Karpov, shook his mighty head. 'It is not so simple, my friend. Before the war ended, the Germans had discovered the atomic bomb, and we know that six were manufactured and hidden on the Continent. Last week, both the Russian and the American Embassies received this note.' Karpov opened his briefcase and brought out a piece of paper, which he read out in a low voice. '"The German High Command, acting on orders from Adolf Hitler, have planted six atomic devices in strategic sites. They can be detonated by remote control." It would seem that, in 1954, there will be a new wave of determination to bring about a revival of the Third Reich.' Karpov stopped. 'At first we treated the whole idea as some sort of hoax. Now we don't think so—that is why we cannot go barging into this place Hawsbortem Towers until we know where these devices are secreted.'

There was a long silence, broken only by the frantic breathing of one very bewildered Prime Minister. After what seemed to be a positive aeon, Kantor spoke.

'We have a chance—a slim one but, nevertheless, a chance. From what this poacher guy saw before he escaped, it would seem that by some strange quirk of fate, Hitler has fallen in love with his so-called son-in-law.'

The Prime Minister leapt to his feet. 'Look here, old man,' he yelled, 'I know that we British are a funny lot of sods at times, but this is going too far . . . He may have been all things, old Adolf, but a queer? Never!'

Kantor held out a soothing paw. 'Let me finish. This Peregrine Oswald was wearing one of Eva Braun's frocks at the time, and Hitler genuinely mistook the lavender for a girl. Now this might help us . . . Rodney, tell the Prime Minister about your idea.'

Rodney brushed a length of cigarette ash from his trousers and, with hands in a position of prayer, began in his well-modulated voice—the voice that had in the past removed obstacles to sexual coupling—to tell of his scheme. 'I have a friend, a very good friend, who is willing to go over the wall, the same wall that Crafty George the poacher used in his escape. It's not a closely guarded part of the house, and we foresee no difficulty. Once inside Hawsbortem Towers, my friend will contact this pouffe chap, and will instil in him the need to gain Hitler's confidence and find out where the atomic devices are hidden. Meanwhile, we will have in the area two divisions of troops—with artillery.'

The four men nodded without enthusiasm. At best it was not much of a plan, but it was worth trying. The men left the office, leaving only the Prime Minister sitting dejectedly in Wainwright-Baggshot's chair, his mind awash with the possibility of sneaking out of the country at Fleetwood and getting a deck-chair attendant's job in the Isle of Man.

The Institution,
Miresea-on-Crouch
May 4th

Dear Mr Dawson,

Do you think that a newspaper would be interested? I can see the headlines: PEREGRINE OSWALD REVEALS ALL! AUNTIE'S ATOMIC EXPLOITS!!

I don't know how people get their stories in the papers. Does it cost a lot? I'd be grateful if you would tell me the Editor's address.

Yours excitedly,

Amy Pluckett (Miss)

Amy Pluckett (Miss)

Extract from a memorandum to my publisher, dated May 6th

. . . I have a proposition. A strange story has come my way, telling of how Hitler survived the war, and how a member of a Top Family was unwittingly caught up in his subterfuge. I think it is probably an extremely saleable idea . . .

The Mansion,
Lytham St Anne's
May 7th

Dear Miss Pluckett,

I've read the last section of Peregrine Oswald's diary, and upon reconsidering the idea I don't think the British public is ready to read this kind of thing in a family newspaper. But do let me see any more you come across.

Yours faithfully,

Les Dawson

Les Dawson

THERE IS no longer the need for Hitler to disguise himself as Mrs Gruber. In fact, all the so-called Gruber family are now walking or marching about with uniforms on, with those awful swastikas sewn on the sleeves. My papa never leaves his room, only empty gin bottles actually vacate his chambers. As for Mama, despite the constant rifle drill and hostage-shooting, she drifts around as if nothing has changed.

And me? Well, fortunately, Adolf sobbed on my shoulder one evening and confessed that he was impotent; and so, up to now, he has merely lavished embraces upon me, but allows me to sleep alone. How long this idiotic farce will continue, I have no conception whatsoever. Eva Braun, whom I married as Greta Gruber, is busy bedding her troops with enormous gusto and doesn't appear to have missed me one whit.

The days are spent holding hands with Adolf and, on rare occasions, he demands that I tickle his feet with a goose plume. To me he tells all his dreams of world conquest—with me at his side, naturally. I want for nothing. When I asked for clothes, he despatched a cavalcade on a buying spree, and my wardrobe is a minor sensation of gold lamé dresses and fur stoles, not to mention the most appealing of underwear. Sometimes I think that if I ever survive this nightmare, I will be able to earn a substantial living as a female impersonator in the East End pubs.

This was the mode of my existence, until that fateful day a week ago, when I was strolling in the vegetable garden and listening to Adolf recite poetry; we were both startled to observe an elderly lady hurtle over that very wall on the other side of which Crafty George had refound his freedom. Adolf and I rushed over and helped the old matron to her feet. She was a frail and aged dowager type, who smelt vaguely of country flowers and cordite. As we lifted her up, she placed something in the palm of my hand; while Adolf tended to her, I stole a glance at the contents of this note. A sharp thrill ran through me as I perused the piece of paper. It read simply: 'Say that I am your Auntie Maude. It's vital for the sake of your country.'

Swiftly, I rammed the paper into the hem of my blouse and rejoined Adolf, who by this time was asking the woman who she was and what she was doing.

'Wait a jiffy,' I said. 'Why, if it isn't my old Auntie Maude from Weymouth.'

Hitler looked at me, puzzled. 'Do you know this frump, my darling?'

'Yes,' I countered with growing confidence. 'It is my dear Auntie Maude. How are you? What on earth are you doing here?'

The geriatric female fumbled in her bag and pulled out a very ornate ear trumpet, which she screwed into her ear. 'Is that really you, my dear niece? Thank heaven you are all right, my dear. I've been so worried about you.'

I shouted in return, 'Oh, I'm fine, auntie. Let me introduce you to my friend—Mr . . . Mr Alfred Hinkler.'

Hitler bowed and kissed her hand. 'Charmed to meet you. Doreen has told me so much about you,' the tyrant said politely.

Doreen had been the first name to spring to mind when he discovered me; now I wished I had taken my time and called myself Jeanette or Ramona, anything but Doreen . . . it seemed so working-class. I asked Adolf to let me take Auntie Maude up to my room for some tea and he nodded in agreement, saluted briskly, about turned, and fired his Luger at a cat who had just done something appalling up a lupin stem.

Once in the safety of my room, Maude told me that I must find out where certain atomic devices were being kept; that I had to do anything in order to learn where they were. We were so deep in conversation that I failed to notice the bedroom door being opened; in stalked a big, muscular, German soldier who was obviously the worse for drink. I knew him—he had tried to make love to me on the landing of the West Wing one night, and I had only got away from him by promising myself to him later in the week . . . He hadn't forgotten and now he was here for his reward . . . and what a shock that lad would get in the process. He lumbered towards me, pushing Maude out of the way. I was about to protest at such cavalier fashion when, to my great amazement, Maude leapt on to his back, put a length of piano wire around his bull neck, and calmly strangled him.

I fainted away at the sight of the murder, and came to with a ewer of water poured on my face by Maude.

'Where can we put the dead Jerry?' she whispered, her lips shining with spittle.

Somehow, I found a vocal cord that wasn't paralysed, and pointed to a section of wall near the fireplace. She helped me to my feet and I tottered over and pressed an ornate wooden lion's head—the entire panel groaned ajar, revealing the secret passage. Maude did an excited jig. 'Marvellous . . . I've always adored secret passages,' she breathed. Together we dragged the huge dead German into the musty darkness of the passage and left him there.

Back in my room, Maude made some tea, and I stopped trembling. I couldn't believe what I'd just witnessed: a frail shaky old woman killing a muscular giant of a man in the prime of his life.

'Did you have to kill him with that piano wire?' I managed to croak. Maude smiled.

'Oh, deary me, no . . . I could have used this, or that I suppose.' From her bag, she produced a gun, a knife, a dreadful-looking rubber cosh and an open razor. She smiled as I grew pale. 'I'm too old for karate,' she said sadly, and with that she broke my chest of drawers in half. Maude shook her head. 'It hurts my hand these days. I have a touch of rheumatism in my fingers, you know . . . Still, it's all part of growing old.'

My mouth was open like Fingal's Cave; none of the past events had sunk in at all. I longed to dance in meadows with my flute, away from all this.

It was only the beginning. During the next few days, I took Maude through the network of hidden passages and the years rolled off her. She revelled in it all, and her enthusiasm was catching; so much so that we even played hide and seek.

One day, we both tiptoed from the passage and into the main dining hall, only to find a pair of Germans in conversation. I indicated to Maude that we should retrace our steps back into our hidey hole, but she merely smiled, crept up behind the two Germans, and cut their throats with a Bowie knive. Once again, after gagging at such slaughter, I was compelled to help her drag the bodies into the passage.

Dear reader, within four days Maude had butchered five more soldiers, and a harlot brought in from Halifax. Adolf, stroking my wig one night as we sat on the fireside rug, told me that he was very worried about the missing men. I suggested that they had deserted, and he agreed, rose to his full length and gave an hour-long speech on the subject of loyalty to the Third Reich. I plied him with strong ale and, as I massaged his toes, said: 'Dear Adolf, can we really beat the Russians and the Americans? After all, there aren't many of us, are there?'

Hitler cocked one eye at me and murmered. '*Meine kleine fraulein*, I have the means to defeat them, fear not.' Shortly after that statement he dozed off fitfully. I still continued to massage his rank feet and kept on whispering to him: 'How can we beat our enemies, dear, dear Adolf?'

He moved restlessly, and words—all in German—tumbled from his lips: '*In . . . der . . . zimmer fur herren . . . Doreen . . . ah bahnhof, ein ist.*' He trailed off, and I risked opening his mouth and pouring a little more ale down his throat. He burped loudly, and commenced to murmur: '*In der gross, gross stadt . . . ha ha bald . . . New York . . . Boom.*'

I hadn't the foggiest idea what the old dictator was on about but I memorised his ramblings, stole out of the room and shot upstairs to tell Maude; she, predictably, was disembowelling a German in the armoury. Once again we lugged the inert Prussian into the secret passage, and laid him alongside his comrades, who by now were becoming odorous.

Back in my bedroom, I told Maude what Hitler had said and, with her help, wrote down most of the garbled account. Later that night, Maude and I crept upstairs into one of the garrets, heaved ourselves through a door in the ceiling, and found ourselves atop the garret, crouching behind the crumbling battlements. From her veritable Pandora's Box of a bag, the incredible geriatric fished forth a signalling lamp, and began to flash Adolf's meanderings to someone out in the woods. I thought I saw some sort of answering flicker from the trees; at any rate, Maude seemed satisfied, and we retreated back to the comparative sanctuary of our respective bedrooms.

It took me some time to drop off—my nerves were a-jangle—and on one occasion, to my horror, I heard Auntie Maude whisper, 'Go to bye-byes, you little German trooper, you.' This was accompanied by the sound of steel thrusting into something soft, followed by a burbling moan.

I pulled the bedclothes over my head as I heard the sound of the panel leading to the secret passage open, and Maude dragging something large into the gaping maw. I wasn't to know that, as sleep wreathed my brow, Rodney Barton and Sam Kantor were decoding information from the message we'd flashed to them and the excitement caused by it would transmit across the Atlantic and begin a chain of events that would eventually save the present civilisation from the New Order. While all this was happening, I was wading through a mire of bad dreams, in which Maude was cutting everybody's head off, and Trevor was in bed with Hitler.

Extract from memo to publisher, dated May 15

Thanks for your phone call. I'll think about it . . .

More news—it's surprising what you hear backstage. I was doing this big show the other night, and an ancient comic (no names, no pack drill, but his jokes have even more whiskers than he has) told me about something he'd been mixed up in New York in 1953. Is this the missing link? Would it make a difference to you?

Extract from memo from publisher, dated May 17

. . . and if your ancient comic is who I think, then he is indeed the Missing Link. Any more news from Miss P?

We're still punching our calculators . . .

GRAND CENTRAL Station in New York. A vast hub with rails of steel issuing forth like the spokes of a bicycle . . . Hordes of tired, complaining soiled commuters, rushing for connections, pushing, cursing amid the boom of the loudspeaker announcements. Businessmen, drop-outs, derelicts, pickpockets, young lovers prised apart, old lovers rekindling the flames. Human energy and sweat. Headaches and calf strain. Busy, frantic and ant-like.

One of the busiest of all the station's sectors: the Gentlemen's Rest Room, situated near the grinding escalator. Lines of men with brimming bladders, fumbling with zips for blessed relief. It was a normal late afternoon.

John C. Buckner in dark grey suiting strolled in casually, and took up the position he had been allocated that morning, during the FBI briefing held at the hotel. He glanced up from his newspaper and looked at his fellow agent, Clark Rosenfield, who was sitting having a shoe-shine. Three other veteran FBI field operatives were lounging close by, waiting for the given signal.

They were taking a calculated chance, based on the garbled message sent from England: the atomic device was hidden somewhere in the rest room. Top men in the States had decided that Hitler's words had meant 'In the gent's room at Grand Central Station one is there'.

Through the portals of the rest room strode a short thick-set man—Harry Rainor, second only to Hoover himself. He stood in one of the stalls and waited until the urinal was empty; he blew on a whistle and the door to the rest room was closed by Clark Rosenfield. All the agents pulled out pistols, and Harry Rainor walked swiftly towards the cubicle where towels were kept. He ordered the attendant, a tall gangling man, out.

The man came out but he had a machine gun in his hand, and he ripped Harry Rainor apart. The shoe-shine boy shot Clark Rosenfield in the stomach before John C. Buckner killed both him and the attendant. Without a word, Buckner ran to the far tiled wall and knocked three times on it, then stood back. The sound of a drill echoed harshly and, within minutes, a gaping hole appeared and several men in blue overalls shuttled in. John C. Buckner spoke crisply: 'Get to it, men, take the place apart if you have to. Remember at all times—this operation must not, I repeat *not*, go outside of these walls.' The FBI technicians nodded and began to take up the floor and break down anywhere that could conceal the device.

The remaining agents examined the dead attendant and shoe-shine boy; each of them had tattooed on the upper arm the slogan *'Hitler Wohnt''* . . . Hitler Lives.

Buckner looked at his companions and said, gratingly, 'The tip-off was right— and it cost two good men.' One of the technicians shouted across to Buckner: 'Found it, John. It's primitive—but Jesus H. Christ, it could turn half of New York state into powder.'

The men gazed down at the device with something akin to awe: what might have happened if the enemy had had more time? The device was hustled away through the hole in the wall, and the rest room was sealed off for a very long time.

Hoover heard John C. Buckner in silence. When the agent had finished his report of the event, he sat back and barked: 'I want a complete news blackout on this. Furthermore, nobody outside this office must know what happened; otherwise, our contact in England will have blown his cover, and that will be the end of it.' He dismissed the men with a wave of his hand and they obediently turned to leave.

As he reached the door, John C. Buckner paused and asked his chief softly: 'Do we have any idea who the contact is in England?'

Hoover looked up and snarled, 'Yeah. He's a fag—what the British call a pouffe.''

As the door closed behind him, Buckner thought, 'Old Hoover's sure got a funny sense of humour.'

News that the device had been found was sent to England; and Sam Kantor hugged Barton in sheer delight.

Dear Mr Dawson,

I must at last admit all: my day is bleak and dreary unless I see your spacious handwriting on an envelope, and know that you have touched it, have even licked the stamps.

I send you a few pages at a time, knowing that a gentleman of your breeding will always answer a lady.

Please let me know that you have received this instalment of Peregrine Oswald's memoirs. Every letter you write brings me joy unbounded

Yours ever,

Amy Pluckett (Miss)

Amy Pluckett (Miss)

The Mansion,
Lytham St Anne's
May 21st

Dear Miss Pluckett,

Your letter alarms me. Are you sure you've been writing to the right person all this time? I can spare a bit of biro, an envelope and a second-class stamp—but that is all I can give towards your happiness.

Les Dawson

Les Dawson

Sir Peregrine Oswald Potts-Belching's memoir

ADOLF HAD been in a foul mood for days. Nine members of his miniature army couldn't be found . . .

Yes, Auntie Maude was still at it, and the secret passage

was more like a charnel house now, but Adolf's main concern appeared to be the reaction of the British public to the outbreak of strikes that were bringing the country to a standstill.

Daily he would rant to me as I sat knitting a sweater: *'Gott in Himmel!* Why are the British still carrying on as if everything was normal, hey? There is a dock strike, a transport strike, a miner's strike . . . There is very little food in the shops, and it is still on ration—and yet, the blind pigs do nothing about it.' One Monday, he kissed me lightly on the cheek, ran his hand down my thigh, then left with two hundred men to invade Poole and Bournemouth.

I was about to make myself a cup of scented tea before rinsing my hair—which had grown so long, I had no need of Eva's wig any more—when Auntie Maude beckoned me into her room. She was drinking from a bottle and standing on the inert body of yet another of her victims . . . this one had a pair of pruning shears sticking out from his chest.

'Oh, Auntie Maude,' I spluttered faintly. 'You can't keep on doing this. Before long, nothing will move any more in the Towers. You really should curb yourself.' With the automatic skill bred of experience I dragged the stiffening cadaver into the secret passage, and propped him alongside his other mates.

On my return, Auntie Maude told me about the finding of the atomic device in New York, and how British Intelligence was relying on me for help. The gist of Auntie Maude's message was that I must glean more information from Hitler as to the whereabouts of the other atomic horrors the Germans had stashed away. We had tea and crumpets later on, and I read her a poem by Longfellow and she fell asleep. I crept away to my own room and played my flute for an hour and had a little weep over Trevor.

I had a nice fire going in the room that Adolf and I used as a private salon, I had prepared a dish of coleslaw for him when he returned from his invasion, and I had purloined a magnum of fine old port—the sort that Adolf liked and the type that appeared to loosen his tongue. I had just taken my apron off, when he shouldered his way into the room in a dreadful temper.

For almost half an hour, he strode about the place ranting at the Poles, the Russians, the Jews, the Americans the price of eggs . . . Finally, he flopped into his favourite chair, set me on his knee and told me what had happened.

Adolf, at the head of his small army, had marched into Ruff-on-the-Ole and commandeered six farm lorries and a Morris saloon car. Then, the column trundled off to invade Poole, stopping for long intervals to mend punctures and shift herds of cows blocking the way. They had reached the delightful little harbour just after lunch, and had been mistaken by the inhabitants for part of a gala procession on its way to the annual Morris Dancing Festival. Within two hours, the beer they had been proffered had proved too strong for Hitler's storm troops, and they had finished up in a pub singing 'The Cornish Floral Dance' with some ardent yachtsmen from Cowes.

But worse was to come: Adolf, who had been trying to speak from the top of the Morris saloon, had been dragged along to a square gaily decked with buntings, and he had been awarded first prize in a fancy dress competition . . . as Hitler. Each time he had screamed that he *was* Hitler the Deliverer, roars of laughter went up, and a theatrical agent from London offered him a week's booking in Rhyl.

Realising at last that it was hopeless, Adolf had his men thrown back on to the lorries, and he had struggled his way home. After telling me all this, he drank deeply of the fine old port, stretched his length on the couch, and fondly indicated to me that I should take his boots off and tickle his feet with my plume. Saucily, I got him to finish half the bottle of port before sending him into raptures with the feather. He lay there breathing heavily as the plume dodged in and out between his aromatic toes.

Softly I began to croon to him: 'Never mind, my dear one. It will all come out right for you, don't worry. After all, you have Something they don't have.'

He smiled and whispered dreamily: '*Ach, mein lieber* . . . I am so lucky that I found you . . . Soon, we make love. You might think me an old man, but my dearest child, I am vibrant. And when you see your old Adolf naked, you will be very surprised at what you see.'

I thought to myself impishly, 'When you see me with nothing on, you're in for one hell of a shock—never mind a surprise!' On I crooned, 'You'll soon be the ruler of the world, dear Adolf. Just relax, my darling warrior.'

He soon began to drift into a light drowsy limbo where I held him with my sing-song urgings, and the application of droplets of port which I infused through his teeth. He rambled on . . . 'Ruler of the world, ja . . . the ultimate weapons . . . ha ha ha . . . New York soon . . . *Boom*. Then those French bastards . . . Paris . . . *Boom*.'

My heart stopped for a moment. Paris? 'Oh, mighty Adolf,' I drooled. 'I would love to go to Paris, but where in Paris would you take me?'

He stirred and coughed as I forced more port down his gullet, at the same instant tickling his big toe with my feather. 'Where in Paris, my Doreen?' (Thank God I thought, he's speaking English; frankly, the Germanic tongue always sounds to me like somebody breaking wind in the bath.) Hitler grinned inanely and went on: 'Where in Paris? Why we must visit the Louvre. Behind the smile, soon *Boom*.' With that, the rabid old despot's bottom set fell out and he fell into a deep sleep.

I crept out of the room to find Aunt Maude and inform her of Hitler's remarks, which meant nothing to me whatsoever. I found her lying in wait on the minstrel's gallery with a brass urn in her hands, watching a burly soldier coming into range. I tried to shout out; but my throat was dry, and I watched in horror as the huge urn crashed on top of the unwary Nazi, crushing his skull to pulp. Aunt Maude did a little jig of delight at her accomplishment and ran down the stairs like a dervish. Once again, together, we towed the carcass into the secret passage. Aunt Maude had a mop and she carefully sponged away the pool of blood on the stone floor of the hall, so that no evidence of the assassination would be found. I found myself admiring the creaking murderess more and more; she was nothing if not utterly efficient. Aunt Maude then slid away to contact British Intelligence, outside in the woods, and I made for my room, to ease my disturbed senses with a snatch of Ravel's 'Pavane pour une infante défunte' upon my flute. But no sooner had I stolen back into my

51

bedroom when the door was flung open, and in staggered Eva Braun, much the worse for drink and bent on trouble-making.

'What the hell are you doing dressed in women's clothes?' she snarled, her face contorted with evil. 'Take them off, do you hear me? Now!'

I found the strength to vault over the bed and cower in a corner, but it was in vain. The awful harpy was on me in a trice, ripping off my dress. Soon, I was absolutely starkers; picking up a chair, she wrenched one of the legs from it and started thrashing me with it. I screamed and wriggled with the pain of the bludgeoning, but she was a positive fury and my struggles only served to incense her. I managed to roll towards the fireplace, and without thinking too clearly I grabbed a handful of soot from the chimney and threw it at her. Fortunately, it caught her in the eyes, and she teetered back on her heels, her hands scrabbling at her face. I rose to my feet, my entire body a pillar of agony, reached the bedroom door and fell into the arms of Aunt Maude. Hoarsely, I told her what had happened and she motioned me to get behind her.

Eva recovered her composure and her rage was a towering furnace of hate. She came slowly towards Aunt Maude, who simply stood in her path, clutching her handbag. Eva growled and made to push Maude out of her way; Maude didn't seem to do anything, but the next minute Eva was flat on her back with her throat cut.

Maude brandished the open razor in Eva's face and scolded her. 'Tut tut, how dare you try to harm my little Oswald, that's a very naughty thing to do.' She took out a pistol from her bag, casually fitted a silencer on the end, and fired a shot into Eva's heart.

Once again, having selected and donned another dress from my wardrobe I helped Maude to stow a corpse in the secret passage. After that, events got the better of me, and I threw up in a basin. After Aunt Maude had made a cup of tea, I broke down in her arms and begged her to get me away from Hawsbortem Towers as soon as possible.

She soothed my brow with her tiny gnarled hands and gently chided me. 'Now, Oswald my dear, you can't go yet.

Britain needs you.' That night she put me to bed with a teddy bear that she had once bought in Woolworth's, and sang me to sleep. As I began the descent into the arms of the Sandman, my last thoughts were of Trevor and the days we had spent together.

Would this present nightmare ever end? I cuddled the teddy bear and quietly wet the bed.

The Institution,
Miresea-on-Crouch
May 24th

Dear Mr Dawson,

(Or may I call you Les now?) Last night I was so happy, I danced for joy. What woman would ask for more than the occasional scrawl sent by second-class post? My skipping feet led me back to that source of all knowledge, the thicket . . .

When I was a filing clerk, I used to tear things up before I threw them away. I think it's shameful the way people carry on nowadays, letting everyone in on secrets.

Yours, till the stars cease to shine.

Amy Pluckett (Miss)

Amy Pluckett (Miss)

ps I never liked the way Buster Keaton pouted. There's never smoke without fire.

Lytham, May 26th

Dear Miss Pluckett,

No time to write. Hope this finds you as it leaves me. Flabbergasted.

Les Dawson

L.D.

JUST OFF Rue Michel and Boulevard St Germain is a small winding street called Rue Monsieur Le Prince. It is a typical Parisian street, smelling of cheap wine and faulty plumbing. Down it, students from the Sorbonne stroll hand in hand, gazing into each other's eyes, old men sit on stools in narrow doorways, and relive the dreams of their past, and scented ladies bemuse the libido. In that street, there are cramped bistros and cellar clubs; there are tiny apartments hiding in large paint-peeling facades that escort the street down to the metro, Odéon. Paris—feminine and alluring, beautiful and cold.

In a nondescript building that lay in a back cul-de-sac off Rue Monsieur le Prince, four men sat in an office that had on the door the legend 'M. Lateur, Curios'. It was in fact, a front for a branch of the French counter-espionage bureau; and Lateur, a small portly man, was the head of the department.

Lateur sat and listened to Sam Kantor and his colleague, Ivan Karpov, in utter amazement. The news that Adolf Hitler was alive and active in Britain had come as a complete shock to him; and the news that an atomic device was secreted in his beloved capital had floored him.

'Believe me, Georges,' said Kantor quietly, 'before the Third Reich collapsed, the Germans had mastered the manufacture of the atomic bomb. The one we found in New York could have destroyed a large tract of North America; and now our informant says that here in Paris is yet another device. Obviously we cannot move in on them in Britain unless we have neutralised these devices beforehand.'

Georges Lateur listened in silence, then finally found his voice. 'But where, my friend, is this weapon?'

Karpov cleared his throat and spoke urgently. 'We have reason to believe that the device is hidden in the Louvre, behind the painting of the Mona Lisa.'

Lateur sat back, appalled. 'How in heaven's name, *mon ami*, do you arrive at that conclusion?'

Kantor told Lateur about Peregrine Oswald's conversation with Hitler; and even to his own ears the story sounded absolutely ridiculous.

When he had finished, Georges Lateur shook his head slightly and remarked with feeling, 'this Oswald, he must be a very brave man indeed, no?'

Kantor looked long at the French chief, and decided not to give out any more information about Peregrine Oswald. How could one begin to describe a man dressed as a woman who had charmed Hitler into taking him as a possible lover? How could you impart data on a person who played a flute, lived in a library and was a pouffe to boot? Kantor shuddered inwardly and decided to keep his informant's character out of it. At 2 p.m. on Tuesday afternoon, despite many protests from tourists, the Louvre was closed to the public, and the Sûreté moved in and formed a cordon about the old palace. Under the leadership of Lateur and Kantor, three teams of specialists began to work. First, the priceless paintings were removed, and then the wall was systematically demolished. Within five minutes an astonished Lateur stood looking down at a metallic grey box secreted within the cavity of the wall.

So engrossed was the team in their discovery that they failed to hear the footsteps behind them. Too late, one of Lateur's men looked over his shoulder, and his warning cry was stilled by a bullet that ripped into his throat. Two men in the uniform of Louvre guides blazed away with autometic pistols, and four French policemen died before these two assassins were shot to ribbons. As in New York, the dead assailants had the words 'Hitler wohnt' tattooed on their upper arms.

Lateur sat down heavily. 'All this time, hey? Just waiting for them to set the thing off. When I think how blind we have all been!' He stopped and shook his head, and Kantor, bleeding slightly from cuts about his face, placed his hand sympathetically on the Frenchman's bowed shoulders. As in the New York discovery, a complete blackout on the finding of the atomic device was immediately imposed. There was, however, one victim of the affray that would have taken some explaining: Mona Lisa had a gaping hole in her mouth where a bullet had entered, and a piece of shrapnel had left a mark on the enigmatic lady's left eye, so that it appeared she was squinting intently. Lateur viewed the damage, and summoned Karpov: the two men whispered hastily together, then Karpov made a frantic phone call to Russia. The world's press was told that the painting was on a long loan to Moscow.

Kantor lit a cigarette, and mused with optimism that they now had two down and four to go. . .

The Institution,
Miresea-on-Crouch
May 30th

Dear Mr Dawson,

I won't call you Les if you don't want me to.

I long to hear from you again.

Reluctantly, I part with another few pages of Sir Peregrine's diary. Please write soon.

Yours alone,

Amy Pluckett

Amy Pluckett (Missing you)

ps I've always wanted an ostrich for a penfriend. Are they house-trained?

Sir Peregrine Oswald Potts-Belching's memoir

THE ATMOSPHERE in Hawsbortem Towers was akin to that usually found in a mouldering crypt. Adolf went about the place like a madman, flecks of spittle dripping from his lips; haranguing all and sundry, including me, and generally being beastly. The disappearance of Eva Braun plus yet another three of his henchmen, had thrown him into such a state that Maude even stopped killing people for a week, in case old Hitler went over the top.

It wasn't only his vanishing army that worried him; we had sightseers trying to peer over the walls in an effort to get a glimpse of Hitler because, by now, news of his re-emergence in Dorset was rapidly spreading. Every time Adolf tried an invasion or the take-over of a town, the population was so indifferent that it took the fire out of him. The Nazis who were planted in the various trade unions soon became such anglophiles they started downing tools for longer tea breaks, and four of them joined a local cricket club.

The British were defeating the Fuhrer with the age-old Secret Weapon of the island . . . Muddling Through. Strikes didn't break their spirit, but merely got them talking to strangers. The presence of storm troopers in the village only served to help vicars get more people to attend garden parties; and, for a small fee, some of the storm troopers actually opened the odd flower show.

Hitler sensed that he was losing his grip on the men, hence his foul mood. To add to his troubles, my mama went dotty, and started riding a horse up and down the stairs, where the heaps of manure on the landings caused havoc with the morning rifle drill. Maude kept on urging me to get Adolf fuddled so that he might reveal the whereabouts of the last four atomic devices, but it was impossible to get close to him, and I became very nervous.

How long this state of affairs would have lasted is quite beyond my comprehension, but an incident occurred just before Lent that gave Adolf fresh hope. It all started when two storm troopers were ordered out of the Frog and Elk after cheating at skittles; in retaliation, they crept back during the early hours of the morning and burnt the old inn to the ground. The impact on the village soaks was devastating: en masse, they marched up to the Towers, forcibly overpowered the sentries at the gate, and demanded that Hitler hand over the two culprits to them. Adolf beamed at the rustic mob—at last he had stumbled upon the Achilles' Heel of the British.

He immediately pinned iron crosses on the arsonists and, in return for blind obedience from the villagers, promised them not one, but two, new pubs to be erected post haste.

During the next few weeks Hitler ambushed every dray waggon he could find and, within a month or so, Dorset was devoid of ale. The population grew sullen and restless. This was the moment Adolf had waited for: in return for the full co-operation of the populace he allowed small amounts of beer through his blockade, and soon Dorset was a hundred per cent Nazi. The fight was on with a vengeance.

Whitbread's Brewery was raided and occupied by the Germans, and the hardened drinkers of Cheltenham and Bristol swore allegiance to the Fourth Reich in their hundreds in order to get a drink.

Adolf was delighted, and tried to get me into bed with him. Once again, I pleaded with him to desist in his advances; he agreed, but reluctantly, and I knew that time was running out for me. After a heavy meal, I took his shoes and socks off and tickled his feet with my plume. As before, I plied him with port, and before long the tyrant began his ramblings.

'Ah . . . Doreen, so nice, so nice, *hein*? You are a naughty girl to ask me not to make the love with you, but tomorrow night my little one will be mine.'

I nearly dropped the feather at his words, but I managed to recover and start my oral probings. 'Yes, my Adolf, tomorrow night. But first, more port for my warrior.' I poured a positive bucketful of the stuff down him, and resumed my gentle questioning.

'Soon, my hero, you will have the whole world at your feet,' I crooned to him. 'You, my dear Adolf, conqueror of the earth with your secret weapons.' He smiled a smile that was quite ghastly, and made him appear half-witted, and I took the opportunity of thrusting the neck of the port bottle into his gaping maw.

'Yes, you are so right, my Doreen. I will be the master, thanks to my little toys. Ha ha ha . . . New York, *Boom*. Paris, *Boom* . . . Then, *Boom* goes Moscow . . . Ha ha ha ha ha.' On he cackled.

'Very good, my sweet warrior,' I drooled. 'Moscow, all those awful Russians—let us hope they don't find your little toy.'

Hitler almost purred as he replied, 'Find it? Never! Who would look under the pillow of a noble martyr.' With that, he went out like a light, and that was that.

Auntie Maude seized me as I crept away from the sodden dictator, and eagerly demanded whether I had found out the location of the third device. I told her everything that Adolf had told me; at first she was elated over the news that Moscow housed the weapon, but because the information regarding its actual site was a trifle sketchy, she became cross and prodded me with her ear trumpet before going off to signal the latest piece of information to the agents waiting in the woods. I remained behind, crept into one of the secret passages and played a Syrian lament upon my flute.

Later, I bathed and changed into a tweed skirt and heavily laced blouse, brushed my flowing locks and had a little weep for my defunct Trevor. I had scarcely begun to read my latest Georgette Heyer novelette, when the bedroom door swung open, and Auntie Maude entered.

'Hurry, we haven't much time. My nephew Rodney wants to meet you personally,' she said loudly. Despite my protests, she virtually bundled me into a raincoat, and we crept into our passage, avoiding with care the row of corpses propped up along the wall. With my nerves twanging like banjo strings, we eventually reached the base of the wall over which Crafty George had effected his escape. Much to my astonishment, Maude pushed against a section of the wall and a small, roughly-hewn hole appeared. She helped me through the aperture and, having followed me, turned and shoved the section of wall back into place.

The geriatric scamp positively danced into the dark beckoning wood, whereas I had to pause for breath on two occasions—much to the contempt of the sweet-faced old mass killer. Half throttled by hanging branches and perspiring like a dray horse, I found myself being ushered before several sombre men in regulation grey coats and broad-brimmed hats. Maude kissed her nephew, a tall presentable chap, and he looked me over with enormous curiosity. It was he who broke the silence first.

'Gentlemen, this is Peregrine Oswald Potts-Belching.' One man in the group sniggered, and I heard another burly type whisper: 'What a bloody fruit.'

I swung my curls in an attitude of displeasure, and demanded of Maude's nephew: 'What, may I ask, is the meaning of having me summoned here?'

'Talk to me like that again, and I'll smack your bottom,' said Maude's nephew. I flushed with anger, and a faint lust, but before I could find a suitable retort, he went on: 'My name is Rodney Barton, British Intelligence, and this is Sam Kantor. The names of the other agents here are of no interest to you.' He motioned me to squat down on a log, lit a cigarette and threw questions at me, questions about my relationship with Hitler.

I found myself telling all: about Hitler's fondness for me, how I gleaned the information from him—which caused vast amusement among the other agents when I got to the part about tickling his feet.

Rodney broke in: 'Has he actually—I mean has he—made . . . er . . . love to you? Is he a queer, a bi-sexual?'

It was too much. I sprang to my full height and shouted, 'No, he hasn't. Here I am, risking life and limb for you beggars, and all you can do is make these awful insinuations! How dare you! I . . .'

I got no further. Rodney pushed me on to the wet earth, towered over me, and said ominously: 'We have to know. From what Aunt Maude tells me, Hitler desires you; and it is only a matter of time before he discovers that you are a man and not—as he believes—a girl. If and when that happens, the jig will be up and we will never discover the whereabouts of the other infernal devices the Nazis have planted . . . That is why we must know everything about you and Hitler. The safety of our country, indeed of the whole world, is at stake here. So you will bloody well tell me all, do you understand?'

I nodded dumbly and with an effort of will told him about Adolf's intention to make love to me later on that very night.

Barton turned to the man called Kantor and said in a low voice, 'Just as we expected. Thank God we made plans for such a contingency.' Then he called softly, 'Jane? It will have to be tonight I'm afraid.' From behind the small knot of stern men a willowy girl of my height and weight, with the same colour hair of the same length as mine, came forward. I gasped in surprise—it was almost like looking into a mirror.

'This is Miss Jane Freeman, one of our undercover specialists. She is going into the Towers with you tonight. If necessary, she will sleep with the Nazi swine in order to continue to get information from him. Now this is vital, Peregrine,' he almost spat the name out, 'you have to change places with her before the ruddy old pig finds out the truth. Aunt Maude will help you all she can, but in the end it will be up to you.'

The girl smiled at me, and my stomach turned at the thought of her surrendering to the demands of the wretched Hitler. She put her hand on my shoulder and said in a low vibrant voice, 'I know what you are thinking. But to me, it's all part of the job I have to do.' I shrugged my shoulders, trying to be unconcerned, when in actual fact I was physically drawn to the lovely girl.

Barton dismissed us abruptly and, with Auntie Maude in the lead, Jane and I fought our way through the matted undergrowth and back to the wall. We had no trouble until we reached the door leading to the unused part of the Towers, when suddenly we were challenged by a huge guard who had been hiding behind a bag of fertiliser. Maude kicked him expertly on his kneecap and, as he bent with the pain of it, she delivered a karate chop to his neck. The large trooper sank to the floor in a heap. Jane's face was full of admiration for the old lunatic's actions and, when Maude thrust a knife through his throat for the coup de grace, the lovely young agent beamed her approval and chastised me for throwing up in a lead urn.

Jane and Maude dragged the body to the secret passage, and he joined his stiffened comrades in the musty tunnel. Maude found two identical short nightdresses, and we made our preparations in case Hitler really did want his oats that evening . . . He did.

He strode into the bedroom at eleven o'clock sated with his new victories over the 'Pig-dog Englanders' in the town of Gloucester, where beer had been on ration for a week; finally the spirit of the people had snapped, and they had vowed full co-operation with Hitler in return for supplies of ale. 'Now, my Doreen, tonight is mine . . . I will not take no for an answer.' With that he pulled me on to his knee and started showering me with damp blubbery kisses. 'Off with your clothes, my little one,' he yelled lustily, at the same time hopping about taking his trousers off.

I smiled coyly, and whispered: 'Wait, my prince, I'm shy. I'm going to put my nightie on.' With that, I crept out on to the landing, entered the secret passage, and Jane, looking radiant in her night attire, went into the bedroom. I heard her click the light off, and within seconds, the bed springs were going 'Creak creak' like billyho.

Finally I heard Hitler moan, 'No more . . . *Gott in Himmel*, my Doreen . . . you are *wunderbar*!' On that happy note, I clambered out of the passage, with the other nightdress on, crept into the bedroom just as Jane slipped out of the bed, got in between the sheets and suffered the moose-like snores emanating from Herr Hitler.

The following morning Adolf couldn't do enough for me. '*Mein Gott*, Doreen, what a night . . . and I thought you were inexperienced . . . Well worth waiting for, my *liebchen*,' he said movingly. A knock on the door halted his admiring commentary and, on command, the door opened and a trooper leapt smartly to attention crying, '*Heil Hitler*. The troops are ready for inspection.' Hitler dismissed the soldier, patted me on the cheek, and marched out. I slumped in a chair and a wave of depression flooded over me. I felt that I couldn't take much more.

The Institution,
Miresea-on-Crouch
June 14th

Dearest Mr Dawson,

I cannot bear this silence. Perhaps you want to know more of Karpov and Kantor?

Yours devotedly,

Amy Pluckett

Amy Pluckett (Missed out on everything)

Dear Mr Dawson,

Is Amy being a nuisance?

She's in her thicket now, knitting a Zeppelin heatshield, and she
won't drink her Marmite.

Yours sincerely,

[signature]

Gregory Snow, MD.

IVAN KARPOV and Sam Kantor sat in an office belonging to
the KGB, and poured lengthy amounts of Vodka into plastic
beakers. They were trying to make sense of the information
recieved from Aunt Maude, regarding the whereabouts of the
atomic device. Teams of agents were scouring the city in an
effort to find the device. Karpov had believed that the
message Peregrine had gleaned from Hitler meant the bomb
was secreted either in or near one of the many statues dotting
Moscow. The very wording, 'Under the pillow of a noble
martyr', seemed to the Russian indicative of hiding places in
vast walloping marble erections to Pushkin or obelisks
reminding everyone of the October Revolution.

Without further ado, Karpov had ordered every stone
plinth and statue to be searched. Now, Moscow had a wealth
of headless heroes and cracked torsos lying all over the grim
metropolis. To explain away the damage, an official bulletin
had stated that the destruction had been caused by a
capitalist tourist who'd gone mad with a hammer.

Kantor gazed sombrely out of the window that overlooked
Red Square, and shook his head as he watched the long
snaking queue of ill-dressed Russians waiting silently to pay
homage to Lenin in his grotesque tomb. What sort of a
society was it, mused the American and, as if reading his
thoughts, Karpov broke in: 'Lenin, my friend, changed the

world and one day, his word will overcome the barriers that halt the march of Communism.'

'Balls,' spat Kantor angrily. 'Your system will defeat itself eventually. You may control the bodies of the poor slobs, but everywhere behind your Iron Curtain people are beginning to think for themselves . . . Come off it, Karpov, you enjoyed the capitalist life in Washington. You didn't seem to think it all that decadent when you screwed those broads night after night.'

Karpov sprang to his feet, his face dark with anger. 'So . . . my bedroom was bugged was it? Swines . . .'

Kantor interrupted the incensed Russian. 'What do you expect? From the moment I arrived in Moscow I have known about the two-way mirror in my hotel bathroom, I know about the tapped telephone and what's more, buster, I know about this!' Sam Kantor took his shoe off and prised the heel away, to reveal a tiny metal cannister glued in the cavity. Holding it close to his mouth, Kantor screamed: *Up your ass, Tovarich.*

Karpov wrestled the shoe away from the American. 'You fool,' he yelled, 'you've probably deafened the operative at the other end.'

The two men struggled and punched each other wildly. The noise brought several burly uniformed men into the room, and the combatants were separated. Breathing heavily, the two men glared at each other. 'That's it, ain't it? In this Godforsaken country, you're all mothersuckin' martyrs, just like that guy Lenin lying there . . .'

Kantor stopped and Karpov's mouth dropped open. 'Under the pillow of a noble martyr,' whispered the Russian. 'Of course . . .'

The afternoon saw Red Square cleared of all people and traffic. Large groups of silent men cordoned off the tomb, as inside the musty crypt experts gingerly unfastened the glass canopy that covered the long-stuffed patriot. A Russian demolition officer, his palms sweating, ordered his men to lift Lenin off his bier; then, in a silence so intense it could have been cut into sections with a fish knife, the officer fumbled carefully under the pillow and brought out of its hiding place the primitive Nazi bomb.

Too late, a soldier shouted a warning about a wire he had spotted which led from the device to the corpse of Lenin. Lenin exploded into a thousand pickled pieces; his head rolled away and finally settled atop the heap of charred corpses that had, only moments ago, been highly-trained specialists. When the smoke of the explosion cleared, at least seven men lay dead, and many more were critically injured. The device was taken away, to be detonated in the Urals. Karpov and Kantor, both white-faced at the carnage, left the tomb and a strict news blackout was immediately put into effect. *Pravda* issued a statement that a trade agreement had been reached with the Americans, and a ballet troupe would shortly tour Dakota.

The Institution,
Miresea-on-Crouch
June 27th

Dear Mr Dawson,

My hero! I have always been attracted to strong silent men. Now you no longer write, I am even more drawn to you. If only we'd met in 1954! I will, I *must* know that you are all right. I will call to see you next Tuesday.

Yours in anticipation,

Amy

Amy

Britain: State of the Nation, 1954

BY MID-AUGUST, the whole world finally realised that Great Britain was under the heel of Hitler . . . Not only was the old fool alive and kicking, but he had the population of the sceptred isle in the palm of his hand, and was even gaining adherents abroad to his banner. In Ireland, anybody who worked in England for Wimpey was given a knighthood, and all jokes about the Irish were punishable by being put to death with an overdose of potato salad. England, for the majority, was a Valhalla. He encouraged hooligans to molest football referees on and off the pitch, he brought down the price of beer and pickles, and a ploughman's lunch only cost threepence in Cheshire.

He re-inforced Hadrian's Wall with a damp course, and all girls in dance halls had to give way to the lads, otherwise they were sent to work in Kent picking hops. The wily old dictator avoided all the mistakes he'd made before—he bought his suits from Jewish tailors and sent money to Israel and, as the ultimate show of good faith, he had himself circumcised.

The Boy Scout movement became armoured and the Boy's Brigade were all given Lugers. All licensing laws were abolished, and brothels were given a state grant for expansion. To please the left wing, Buckingham Palace became a bingo hall and union leaders had a room where they could go and worship Wedgwood-Benn. The Royal Family were treated quite decently and were bunged in a council flat in Wapping. The Welsh fought bitterly for their independence, but Adolf won them over in the end by distributing free leeks in Swansea, and making the hymn 'Men Of Harlech' the new national anthem. But what really made the Welsh look upon Hitler as the Messiah was his bright idea of turning Chester into a rugby ground.

The Scots protested at having to wear tartan shorts and braces instead of the kilt; an ambassador was dispatched to see Adolf, who had the man's foot nailed to a plank and tortured the poor Celt by playing a Jimmy Shand record. Nazi money came streaming in from South America, and prices shot up: in fact you couldn't buy a slum in Lambeth for under thirty thousand pounds.

It was, to say the least, a most curious situation, not actually all that unpleasant, especially if one was an alcoholic or a libertine. But, as in the manner of all dictators, Hitler had to find a common enemy for the populace to hate in order for the Fourth Reich to maintain control. He found it, not with any ethnic group, but with . . . teetotallers.

It soon became an habitual sight to witness storm troopers daubing shop windows with slogans like, 'Don't buy from this shop the owner doesn't drink.' There were many ugly incidents to upset sensitive souls: staunch teetotallers were herded together like cattle in concentration camps in Bowness, where they were forced to drink Guinness all day; and, in cases of rebellion, the offender would be made to share a room with either a Methodist or a double-glazing salesman.

The British realised that the rest of the world was re-arming against them, but it didn't seem to matter. After all, Hitler had the Bombs didn't he? So up yours, buggerlugs.

Mob rule was the order of the day. Income tax offices were blown up daily; the Air Force was strengthened with increases in salaries and any woman of your choice, plus for relaxation pilots could have a half day off to go and bomb the Isle of Man.

There was a lukewarm underground movement of sorts, usually run by celibate non-drinking monks, who were hunted down and hung in night clubs. Then Hitler made a grave error of judgement in his dealings with the sturdy British character . . . After storm troopers closed down a working men's permissive sauna and massage parlour in Durham, a riot broke out; and, in the ensuing fracas, a stripper called 'Boom Boom' was shot to death in a lavatory . . . The storm trooper responsible was beaten up and his union card burnt, and ten of his fellows were forced to buy a British-made car.

In retaliation, Hitler ordered the closure of all breweries north of Knutsford; by late September, a state of civil war existed between the North and the South. Adolf went off at the deep end and, using radio to put his threats across, declared that he would explode one of his devices if the North didn't surrender. He got his reply in the shape of a lump of tripe coated with nitro-glycerine.

It was time for the remaining atom bombs to be found and quickly; meanwhile America shipped arms to the Northerners and a new capital city was born: Gateshead, and Vera Lynn did the opening ceremony.

Despite all this mess, the hold Hitler had on Britain didn't seem to abate and, after the battle of Stoke-on-Trent, when Southern forces retreated under the attack from the North, Adolf took council, re-opened the northern breweries and took the sting out of the civil war. It still went on—but free fish and chip shops mushroomed, and the football pools were fixed so that the punters could win a bit, and the Queen was sent out cleaning . . .

                                              The Mansion
                                              Lytham St Anne's
                                              July 1st

Dear Amy,
    Sorry, have been away. I will write you a long letter soon.
    No, don't call on Tuesday—I will be in the Sudan for a charity marathon. And would not the charm go out of our correspondence if we met?
    Let us keep the Post Office busy—and remember, someone, somewhere, wants a letter from you.
    Yours, etc,

    Les

    Les

                                              The Institution,
                                              Miresea-on-Crouch
                                              July 3rd

Dear Mr D,
    Alright.

    Amy

    Amy

The Institution,
Miresea-on-Crouch
July 5th

Dear Les,

I did not mean to be so abrupt. Here is another section of the diary.

Please forgive me?

Yours as always,

Amy

Amy

Sir Peregrine Oswald Potts-Belching's memoir

EVENTS WERE moving so fast I couldn't keep pace with it all. Adolf had issued an ultimatum to the North: surrender within a week, or he would use an atomic device to shake the world into realising that the Fourth Reich was here to stay.

He wasn't in good health—I have no idea what Jane did with him every night, but Adolf looked ghastly. Aunt Maude kept killing off his men, and there was hardly enough room to get past in the secret passages because of all the corpses stacked up against the wall; she was badgering me to get from Adolf the information about where the other bombs were hidden, and it was obviously not going to be easy the way things were shaping up. Frankly, I was at my wits' end wondering how to get Hitler in the right mood; also my emotions were mixed about my feelings for Jane . . . I thought about her constantly, hating her for what she had to do, and loving her for her courage.

It is of a paintbrush that future historians will say: 'That was the turning point.'

It happened one Tuesday morning. I was at a loose end, and old Adolf was in a foul temper, having been informed that another of his stalwarts was missing. I knew where the missing man was alright—dead as mutton in a Priest's Hole, with a length of two-core flex buried around his bull neck. For the want of something to do, I decided to paint a mural on my bedroom wall. I had chosen as my subject Leander emerging from the Hellespont, and became so engrossed in my work that I didn't hear Hitler enter the room. It was only when he fondled my buttocks that I realised there was anybody with me. Startled, I turned around waving the paintbrush; to my complete astonishment, Hitler went rigid and his eyes widened as the brush went to and fro in front of his face. At first I was puzzled by this and then it hit me: Adolf was hypnotised by the paintbrush. After all, he'd started out in life as a painter. It was too good an opportunity to miss, so I carefully—still swinging the brush—began to question him.

'Can you hear me Adolf?' I said nervously.

'Yes, I can hear you,' droned Hitler, his eyes like chapel hat-pegs.

'What does the paint brush mean to you?' I asked him.

His face took on a dreamy expression, with a hint of pride flowing into the hollow cheeks as he replied in a monotone voice: 'I was a great painter . . . three rooms in undercoat, two hours, no lunch break,' he breathed wistfully. 'Once I painted a Bavarian bungalow in three days for Fraulein Muller; white walls, shutters done in non-drip autumn green.'

I took the bull by the horns. 'Where are the other secret weapons hidden, Adolf?' He smiled like a child with a rusk. 'One in New York, one in Paris, one in Moscow . . .'

I butted in. 'Oh, we know about those, dear heart, but where are the others?'

Hitler answered in a sort of sing-song chant. 'One in Rome . . . ha ha . . . visitors actually throw money on top of it and make wishes . . . Soon *der big bang*.'

'Clever old Adolf,' I whispered. 'Now, tell me where the others are.'

He put his finger in his mouth. 'Ha yes . . . the other ones, all my babies. Well, one is in foggy London Town under the Player's Theatre in Villiers Street . . . Soon, *Boom*.'

My pulse raced. 'Is that all your babies?' I asked him.

'Oh no, *mein* Doreen, nice little Doreen, no I have one more, and that one is . . .'

He never finished the sentence, because at that moment the door swung ajar and knocked me to the floor. I dropped my brush and Hitler came back to his senses. A large purple German was standing to attention in the doorway. 'Heil Hitler,' he screamed, and I heard his dentures click audibly.

'What is it?' growled Hitler, shaking his head as if to clear it.

'British forces in the North send message from Bolton. No surrender!' Hitler railed and ranted, struck the big German across the face, and stormed out in a shower of spittle.

I ran to Aunt Maude's room where she was preoccupied with the task of disembowelling a storm trooper pegged out on the carpet. I fought the waves of nausea that threatened to engulf me, and passed on the information. At her bidding, once again I assisted her in dragging the carcass into our well-stocked secret funeral parlour. Having accomplished the grisly task, she went off to signal to Rodney Barton in the woods, returning soon to order me to accompany her to see Barton.

There was a lot of activity going on in the grounds of the Towers, and it took some time to creep out from the hall. Barton and a sombre tense group of men were waiting for us, and much to my surprise, a beefy type in a uniform shook me warmly by the hand and said in a pompous voice: 'Well done, Mr Potts-Belching, our country owes you a debt of honour.' I stammered something or other in response, and the atmosphere relaxed.

Barton addressed me next. 'Only one device left for us to find. From what you gleaned from Hitler, we know that the Trevi Fountain in Rome is the location of the Italian device; and of course, the hiding place in London is self-explanatory. How in Heaven's name did you get the old brute to divulge the information?'

I meekly told them about the effect the paintbrush had on Adolf and, after the summary, the group stood stunned. Quickly recovering himself, Barton filled me in what was happening in the country. The North had been told discreetly to cool it, and to make out that they would consider disarming; this news would lull Hitler into believing he had won, and therefore he would not make plans to detonate the remaining atomic bombs. Hawsbortem Towers was being closely watched, all road movements were being monitored for German troops infiltrating into the suburbs of London, and the whole of the Western world was ready to pounce and destroy the birth of the Fourth Reich . . .

It was heartening news. I asked about Jane, and was curtly informed that her services were still required. My job, I was told, was to get the location of the last device. So Auntie Maude and I went back to the Towers, and Maude promised me she wouldn't kill any more Germans until after tea.

Jane was in Hitler's bedroom, looking utterly adorable in a gossamer gown and my heart thudded at such loveliness. She smiled at me and asked how things had gone with Barton. I gave her a brief résumé of events, all the time finding it difficult to keep from throwing my arms about her. I was in a turmoil of emotion; most of my sheltered life I had been the adored object of Trevor's love, and now I found stirrings for the love of the opposite sex dominating my effete soul.

Jane looked at me quizzically and said softly, 'You've changed, Peregrine. You know that yourself, don't you?'

I nodded, lowering my gaze from her thoughtful face.

She went on, 'Let me help you find your true self.' She rose and came towards me, and I snatched her into my arms and we fell on to the bed. I have only one comment to make about what followed. Trevor was wrong . . .

Jane lay back and her eyes were misty. 'Darling,' she breathed. 'That was too much. Oh darling, I love you.' I held her close, my heart full of my new-found passion. We lost track of time then, suddenly, we heard Hitler's voice shouting out for me . . . Panic-stricken, I dressed myself hastily back into my accursed skirt and blouse, whilst Jane, still naked, pressed the section of panelling on the wall and squirmed through the narrow opening, her delightful bottom making a superb exit.

I tidied my curls and sat on the bed demurely, waiting for Adolf to appear; when he did, I knew I was in for a spot of bother. He leered at me, and within a short time he was naked apart from his jackboots. Without any preamble, he started showering me with kisses more blubbery than one would get from a sperm whale. Ashen with desire, he started to remove my skirt and—to my surprise—I discovered that I was stronger than I had ever given myself credit for being. With ease, I threw him off the bed, and he landed heavily on top of his gold-rimmed chamber pot. It only served to excite him further, and he growled with lust and made another grab for me.

Suddenly I spotted his shaving-brush on the dressing-table. I lunged for it and grabbed it just as he threw his weight on top of me. I held the brush in front of his eyes, and they became glazed as I started to swing it to and fro. I wriggled myself from under him, still waving the lunatic bristles about and, to my relief, Aunt Maude assisted by coming up behind the hypnotised lunatic, and rabbit-punching him into insensibility.

We had to act fast to allay his suspicions when he came round and, to my astonishment, I found myself taking charge . . . It wasn't yet dusk, so Jane couldn't change places with me; I tore off my clothes and aided Aunt Maude to shove Hitler on top of the bed, then I got in between the sheets and waited with bated breath for Adolf to surface. He groaned, rubbed his head, and looked around blearily. Quickly I took the offensive.

'Oh, Adolf,' I moaned, 'don't hurt me again.'

He dropped his mouth like a portcullis. '*Mein* Doreen, was I too brutal? I can't remember what I did . . . my head hurts. What happened?'

I covered my face with my hands. 'You were like an animal . . . a tiger . . . you made love to me, your eyes were savage, your face went blue and when you had slaked your thirst, you passed out,' I whispered.

He was instantly contrite, but obviously proud that I had called him a tiger. 'Forgive me, my little one,' he crooned. 'It will never happen again, this I promise you . . . Funny though, I don't recall giving you . . .' He trundled out of the room, still caressing the back of his head.

I hurriedly re-dressed, opened the secret passage panel, and motioned for Jane to come out. As she did, her nudity took my breath away. She kissed me tenderly, and went off to her own room.

Then the scene of the story switched to Rome, and London . . .

THE ETERNAL City was sealed off at 6.30 in the morning, and agents from America, Russia, France and Italy moved in to defuse the device. Acting on the information passed on by Aunt Maude, the government knew that the device was hidden under or near the famous Trevi Fountain, so beloved by novelists, lovers and water board rating officials. Armed soldiers took up strategic positions in order to thwart any possible attack by fanatical ex-Nazis, and the operation went ahead. By noon, a cry of triumph warbled from the throat of a damp agent as he gleefully pointed to a metal container wallowing in a ragged hole that was situated on the bed of the fountain. A cheer arose from the relieved men and a troop of caterers came over with steaming tureens of spaghetti. Good-naturedly, Sam Kantor bade the men eat, and he and Karpov walked away to a far corner of the site to ponder the next move . . . It was by the Grace of Jehovah Himself that they did so, beacuse the tureens of spaghetti exploded and killed ten agents before the strands finally settled on ledges and disturbed the pigeons.

The smiling chefs who had delivered the deadly pasta had flung themselves to the ground seconds prior to the explosion. Now they rose, removed their long white hats, and produced machine pistols which commenced to spit out a stream of death in all directions. Their fire was returned and, before long, the withering lead from the soldiers and those agents still operative began to take a steady toll among the dedicated Nazis. Suddenly, a smoke bomb was hurled between the combatants and, under the choking mantle, a Nazi raced across to the wrecked fountain, plunged in and tucking the bomb under his arm, made a bolt for cover. He was cut down before he could reach safety, but the bomb was immediately retrieved by another German, who galloped away and flung himself into a small convertible that had stood by with its motor idling over. The car shot off amid the smoke and screams of the thwarted Nazis. Kantor cursed prodigiously and Karpov finished off a bottle of Vodka. Urgent telephone calls were made and roadblocks were set up, seemingly to no avail, because no agent reported the sighting of the car. Helicopters soared into the Rome sky and the hunt was on; also, as Kantor was only too bitterly aware, the security screen was gone. No longer could the operation be kept from the world; and it would be only a matter of time before Hitler heard about the affair, and doubtless, in a fit of pique, he would detonate the remaining devices. The die was cast; the convertible was seen racing for the Austrian border, a helicopter was sent out to keep tabs on the car and Karpov and Kantor agreed that there was only one course of action—blow the car up, and the bomb with it. From information relayed by the helicopter, the location seemed perfect: a mountainous region with a minute population and piles of sheep dung and the odd tenor.

An Italian war plane, one of the few that didn't surrender, circled over the speeding car, and dropped a stick of high incendiary bombs. They promptly blew the car, the atomic device and a vast chunk of the Dolomites into limbo. A team of medics were dropped into the area to evacuate as many people as possible; their instruments showed a very small amount of radioactivity, and that was concentrated mainly in the sheep shit. So at least the device hadn't been 'dirty', but the ominous cloud hovered for quite a period over Lake Cortina and killed off most of the carp.

As the world buzzed over the explosion, Karpov and Kantor held a press conference, and the whole plot was out in the open. The President of America and his Russian counterpart flew to Camp David for urgent consultations and a game of billiards, and a State Of War was declared against Britain. Rodney Barton was ordered to start hostilities against Hawsbortem Towers, and London was cordoned off as soldiers went in to defuse the bomb under the Villiers Street Players' Theatre.

The Players' Theatre was showing its long-running offering, *Ridgeway's Late Joys*, and the audience were singing the old songs lustily and quaffing ale with evident relish. It was a first-class bill: Mr Simon De Vere and his Jumping Infants; Harrison's Catholic Singing Geese; The Chelmsford Madrigal

Society; Mr Winkle Wilson, a dwarf comedian; and, top of the bill, Gladys Boothroyd who recited poems and did a strip-tease in a bucket of ferrets.

Suddenly, the auditorium was filled with soliders and overalled technicians, all grim-faced because the old lady in the box office had made them pay to come in. A large matron from Ohio, whose husband had made a fortune out of eggs, swooned as she watched, open-mouthed, the bustling parade of authority taking charge. Two visitors from Uganda demanded to speak to their ambassador, only to be informed that the government they'd left in power back home had been eaten by terrorists.

Rodney Barton leapt on to the podium and waved his arms for silence. In his commanding voice, he told them to be calm and leave the theatre in an orderly fashion. So well did he put his words across that he received a standing ovation and he obliged by singing a snatch from *H.M.S. Pinafore*.

Soon the theatre was emptied and the search for the atomic device began, all to no avail: dressing-rooms, toilets, beneath the stage area . . . nothing was to be found. All the clothes in the wardrobe and theatrical skips were flung out and examined, floor boards were ripped up, drains unclogged . . . but no sign of the bomb was to be evinced. Barton was now fully convinced that the information had been wrong and he fumed inwardly. Some of the technicians and troops had been offered beer and they took full advantage of the goodwill. Rodney, sipping a pink gin, idly wandered over to the grand piano in the pit and strummed out a tune on it. After the first few bars, a head appeared from beneath the pianoforte.

'Who the hell are you?' barked Barton.

'I'm the resident pianist here, Miss Maria Pringle. When I heard the commotion I was frightened, so I hid underneath the piano.' The owner of the timid voice, on scrutiny, turned out to be a greying lady in a faced velvet dress, plain of facial feature, with horned rimmed glasses atop a wide boned nose. Nervously, she watched Barton resume his strumming, and when his middle digit hovered over top C sharp, she gave a little scream.

Barton turned in surprise. 'What on earth is the matter, my

dear lady? My knowledge of music is quite extensive. In fact, at Eton I was considered a virtuoso upon the bassoon.' With that curt retort, he concentrated his attention once more on the keyboard.

Miss Pringle's face was ashen and everytime top C was threatened by Barton's finger, she flinched. Finally, in the last haunting bars of 'Tiptoe Through The Tulips', Miss Pringle made a grab for Rodney, positioned the startled agent into a 'Flying Mare' and Barton performed a parabola into the front stalls. As he scrambled to his feet, Miss Pringle whipped off her mat of grey hair to reveal a totally bald head. The glasses were discarded, and on the face could now be plainly seen the mark of a duelling scar.

What riveted everybody's attention most was the sight of a machine gun in the awesome creature's hands. 'Pig dog *Englanders*' the erstwhile Miss Pringle shouted. 'Long live Germany . . . *Heil Hitler*.' A stream of lead chattered across the theatre, cutting down the men like a scythe. The short battle came to a halt when a well-aimed hand grenade blew the machine gunner into crumbs of pumpernickel.

Looking down at what was left of the pianist, Barton was sure that he was looking at Alfred Muller, a wanted war criminal who was supposed to have died in a Russian brothel. Rodney looked at the piano and he knew where the device was. Gingerly the piano lid was removed, and fastened to the bottom of the instrument was the bomb with a wire leading to the key of top C.

A tired technician muttered, 'Bloody lucky escape you had there, sir.' Barton nodded dumbly, and vowed to take up a Jew's harp in future.

Sir Peregrine Oswald Potts-Belching's memoir

Auntie Maude told me what had happened in Rome and I had visible palpitation. I ushered Jane into my room, and the three of us put our heads together and drew up plans. I knew that we had little time left to persuade Adolf to divulge the location of the last remaining device, and I was determined to get Jane away from it all. To my surprise, Maude agreed and that very night we started smuggling British troops into Hawsbortem Towers in readiness to seize the place before the main attack. I left Jane with Barton, and I was in tears as she, sweet lass, threw her arms around me and kissed me soundly and emotionally.

'Please be careful, my love,' she whispered in a trembling voice.

Barton overheard her, and with a whip to his voice, declaimed loudly: 'Well, well, the pouffe is changing horses, hey?'

I stiffened with shame, then anger took over and I punched Barton firmly on the chin. To my complete astonishment, he went down like a sack of barley. Several soldiers came rushing over and they grabbed me but Rodney got to his feet, shook his head, rubbed his chin and gestured that I should be freed.

'I asked for that, old man,' he said. 'I apologise to you and to Jane.' He walked away and started to shout orders to the waiting military. Jane looked at me with eyes that sparkled.

'I love you, Peregrine . . . you're quite a man,' she said proudly. Me. A man. Was it so long ago that I would cavort about the lawns with my flute? Did I ever really fling myself into the arms of Trevor? My musings were dismissed by the reality of our situation and, turning to wave a final goodbye to Jane, I raced back through the trees and re-entered the grounds of Hawsbortem Towers.

I couldn't find Hitler anywhere, and so I scoured the place for the potty dictator. I found him jumping up and down in a fit of fearful anger in what had been the drawing-room. Around him, his staff officers were trembling and ashen as he raved, his eyes like hot humbugs. I tidied myself up, hating my shoulder-length hair, and decided to take the bull by whatever you take a bull by.

I marched boldly into the drawing-room. Hitler paused in his rantings and shouted to me. 'What am I to do, *mein* Doreen? I have been betrayed by fools.' I squared my slim frame and said in a controlled voice, 'You must broadcast to the nation, my hero, and then you must show the world that you mean business by pressing the button to send off our little friend in New York.'

Adolf gaped at me, then threw his arms around me. 'Ja . . . it is time for *Boom* in America . . . We go now to the BBC.'

I cut in. 'No, my warrior, it is too dangerous for you to venture into London. Inform the British troops outside, they will obey you. Or let me do it.'

Hitler had tears in his eyes. 'Would you do this for me, little one?' he whooped. I nodded and, out of the corner of my eye, I saw—to my horror—one of his staff officers being strangled by Maude. To keep the attention of Hitler and his cohorts while Maude dragged the expiring Jerry into the secret passage, I stood to attention and started singing 'Eidelweiss'. They all joined in, and soon the room was reverberating to the melodic tune.

Maude was having difficulty shoving the German through the narrow aperture leading to the passage, so as the last strains of 'Eidelweiss' ended, I jumped up on to the table and led the entire assembly into a rousing chorus of 'Deutschland Uber Alles' which gave my creaking murderess enough time to haul the defunct Prussian fully into the priest's hole. Adolf clapped and wept and kissed everybody, including me, and on that happy note I marched out from the drawing-room and into the grounds, where there was sporadic rifle fire taking place. Waving a white flag, I passed through the massive wrought-iron gates of the Towers, and I was met by Rodney Barton.

Quickly, I told him of my plan, which I confess was a somewhat desperate one: it was this. If I could get Hitler to detonate the now defused device in New York, could Barton arrange for all the news media to announce that New York had been destroyed? My hope was that Adolf would be taken in, and then I could pursuade him to reveal where the last device was hidden. Barton gloomily assessed the plan, and grudgingly agreed to go along with it.

I returned to the waiting throng of storm troopers at the gates and, acting on our plan, I solemnly informed Hitler that a broadcast unit was on its way to the Towers. The minutes ticked by in a stifling sombre silence, and Hitler stood alone away from the group, lost in a train of thought. I grew more nervous as we waited. So many things could go wrong . . . would Barton get the orders to all the news media in time?

Would they all co-operate?

Nobody could telephone Hitler now because all the telephone cables were cut; only by radio could he now receive news. I had suggested to Barton that the American news service in London be alerted the first, and possibly they could pretend that the bomb had gone off in the New York rest room. However, that was up to him.

Suddenly, Hitler turned and marched briskly over to me. 'How did they find out about the device we had in Rome, hey?' he said in a puzzled voice. 'I told no one, Doreen, never did I . . .' He broke off, and squinted at me. 'Wait, I seem to think I told you about it, didn't I?' I swallowed heavily.

'You might have mentioned it, Adolf, dear,' I said in reply. He gazed at me for what seemed an aeon.

'How did you know all about the "Little Friends" we have hidden away? Not an hour ago you told me to press the button to blow up New York'.

As he spoke, I was thinking fast. 'Sometimes, my love, when you have spent your passion, you talk in your sleep. But never would I mention a word you have said to me to a living soul.' I answered him with my head bowed.

He was about to reply when the BBC van arrived at the gates; the vehicle was searched and then allowed into the grounds. Technicians fixed up their equipment in the drawing room, and at 7.30 p.m., Adolf Hitler gave his now historic address to the world.

'I have tried to avoid bloodshed, I was lenient in my dealings with the world. I wanted only for the Fourth Reich to rise again and defeat the powers of the Soviets who are out to destroy mankind, but the Western Alliance—fools that they are—did not listen. Now the full strength of the glorious Reich must be demonstrated. In one hour's time, I will detonate an atomic bomb in New York; it will only be the first of such weapons to be used in bringing the whole world to its knees . . . You have only yourselves to blame.' There was a lot more: he went on about the filthy Poles, Catholics, the rotten painters in British industry, and the inferior gloss used on new houses. After he'd finished talking, he abruptly about-turned on his heel and left the drawing-room, closely followed by several austere gentlemen in white coats, who, I guessed correctly, were members of his scientific brigade.

How that next hour crawled by. There wasn't a sound to be heard either in the grounds or the woods. Auntie Maude was busily creeping around, stabbing unwary German with a knitting needle, and then carting them off to God knows where, so I kept well away from her. I sat in my bedroom biting my fingernails down to my wrist, and nearly jumped out of my skin when an enormous German entered the room and informed me that Hitler wanted me in the armoury. This was a room I hadn't spent much time in, and when I arrived I was stunned to find that it now resembled a scientific laboratory.

Adolf smiled at me and crooned proudly, 'Tonight you will stand by my side and see history in the making . . . I'll destroy the world if I have to.' I watched in awe as a tall gloomy man began to count, with his finger pressed lightly on a button that was situated in the middle of a black metal panel. 'Ten, nine, eight, seven, six,' . . . the room was holding its breath, 'five, four, three, two, one. Fire!' He pressed down on the button, and we waited. Adolf motioned to a trooper to turn the radio on.

'Hitler has carried out his threat,' a voice screamed at us from the set. 'New York City is no more. News is filtering in that Manhattan island has sunk. The death rate is . . . oh, my God!' The voice halted. All the Nazis cheered and Hitler did a jig of pure delight. He turned to me. 'Soon they will surrender, *mein* Doreen! Soon America will sue for peace.'

The radio crackled into life; whoever was on the other end was a damn good actor. 'The President of the United States declared a few moments ago that America will fight to the last. Already American troops and aircraft are invading Britain . . . Our Russian allies have pledged to give us all aid.'

Adolf slapped his knee. 'Russia, hey? Ha ha ha . . . press the button for Moscow.' The tall depressed man began another count down, and soon the radio flashes began: 'The insane acts go on. Tass have just reported that another device was exploded in Moscow, no further news is available . . . A curfew is now in force and from Parliament, comes a State of Emergency.'

We hadn't long to wait before the radio came to life again. 'The British government is prepared to meet Hitler to discuss an armistice.' The rest of the bogus newscast was drowned in a veritable roar of triumph from the assembled staff officers, and some even forgot themselves and started to pound the Fuhrer's back. An idea came to me which I knew would appeal to Aunt Maude. Bottles of beer were being opened, someone produced a length of Bavarian sausage, and a celebration was about to take place.

I crept away and sought out Aunt Maude, finding her sitting on the chest of a spreadeagled trooper twisting piano wire around his neck.

'Won't be a jiff,' she cooed. 'This one was a bit of a handful. Help me, dear, hit him over the head.' Closing my eyes, I obeyed by bludgeoning the colossal kraut with a mace that I disentangled from the grip of a suit of armour standing against the wall. I heard the sick crunch of the weapon biting into the head, and was promptly ill. Maude wheezed as the German's neck was nearly severed with the piano wire, and we rolled him through the secret panel and into the passage.

Recovering myself, I informed Maude of my plan: it was right up her street. I merely wanted her to go into the armoury and kill all the scientists there.

I returned to the celebration, where Hitler sat in a chair with a smile of absolute idiocy on his face. I whispered to him, 'Let us go and make love, now, my warrior.'

The old fool sprang to his feet and drooled. I led him away; outside Aunt Maude curtsied to him and winked at me. Adolf and I mounted the stairs like two randy gazelles, and I had to think of something quickly. He streaked into the bedroom and before he'd taken a breath, he was absolutely starkers—except for his jackboots and tie.

He motioned for me to get stripped off, and I seized the opportunity to say, 'Adolf, you were once a master painter, what colour should I do the bedroom?' He roared with laughter.

'*Mein* Doreen, you are so funny. To hell with this room,

soon you will be sleeping in the White House, no? Maybe we decorate the Kremlin in lincrusta.'

I pouted. 'Humour me, Adolf, what would you do with this bedroom?' He launched himself off the bed and strutted towards me, and pulled my skirt off. As his hand started to roam, I picked up the paint brush and wagged it in front of him . . . It worked. His eyes went like glazed cherries, he had an erection and he stood stock still. I left him in that mirth-provoking pose, and shuffled off to see how Aunt Maude was doing . . .

She was doing splendidly. Four scientists were hanging from various assorted light fittings, two were tidily dismembered on the table, all parts carefully numbered, and the last one, the tall sad man who'd pressed the buttons previously, was being slowly choked to his demise with a cucumber that Aunt Maude was tenderly pushing down his gullet.

She looked up at me and beamed. 'What a marvellous time I've had dear boy,' she said as the German's death rattles vibrated the cucumber. I nodded and, clearing my throat, I told her that now was the time for me to get the whereabouts of the last device from Adolf. Instead of humping the slaughtered Nazis into the secret passage, I simply locked the armoury door and threw the key into an urn that contained a most baleful-looking aspidistra.

Maude and I climbed the stairs and entered the bedroom. Adolf was still there in his rampant nudity, and Maude playfully tickled his genitals with her finger. To hide the poor man's fruit, I tied an apron around his middle. It was time to find out where the last device was.

'Adolf, dearest,' I crooned, wagging my brush to and fro. 'Where is the other little *Boom Boom*?' Hitler didn't answer. I tried again—nothing. I gently slapped his face—nothing. I felt his heart beat: it was strong but slow. I tried to bend his knees; again—nothing. He was as stiff as a piece of chipboard. Aunt Maude poked and pinched the cold spare flesh—all to no avail.

Outside the house, rifle fire started up again, and a group of British commandos burst throught the door. With their help, I laid Adolf on top of the bed and put a quilt over him.

Together with the troops, Aunt Maude and I left the bedroom and wended our way out of the house and into the woods.

I told Rodney Barton everything that had happened and he was thunderstruck. 'What the hell do you mean? Is he in a permanent trance?' he said angrily.

I nodded. 'God knows what effect that paint brush had on him, perhaps it finally toppled him off his rocker.'

'Well, there's nothing we can do now about him. No button's been pressed, so it's safe to assume that for the moment we're all right,' Barton replied shortly. He gave crisp instructions to a red-necked high-ranking officer who looked a trifle ga-ga, and artillery shells began to rain heavily on to the Towers. Suddenly I went cold.

'Barton, for pity's sake, stop the bombardment . . . my mother and father are still in the house.' I was mortified. With the excitement, I had forgotten all about them. Barton stopped the salvo, and I raced back into the besieged stately home with trepidation.

The interior of the Towers was an exercise in ruin: bodies lay everywhere in untidy piles, and the moans from the injured sounded like a choir of tone-deaf banshees. I shuddered and tried to avert my eyes from the horrific spectacle. Aunt Maude had followed me inside, and from time to time she bent to scrutinise the fallen Germans; if she found any sign of life, doubtless the old horror would carefully extinguish it.

I scoured the shambles in search of Mama, and found her sitting astride her favourite chestnut gelding. She was dressed in a gold lamé ballgown and she had a battered tiara jammed on her head. As I approached and seized the reins to coax the horse out, she gave me the benefit of one of her celebrated redoubtable glares, and trumpeted: 'Just who are you, young man? Your raiment does not suggest that of an ostler.'

I shook my head. 'Dear Mama, it is I, Peregrine Oswald.' She took a long look at me through her pince-nez.

'Surely not one of the Surrey Oswalds? A family quite beyond the pale. Indeed, did I not once cut Lady Rosemary Oswald from our guest list in Rotterdam? Sorry state of affairs that Punjab business . . . Imagine, Simon Oswald actually riding point-to-point in grey flannel trousers.'

I did not bother to correct her; it was quite apparent that she had retreated into her world of yesteryear and, judging by her glassy expression, I didn't think she would ever emerge from it. Stumbling wildly, I managed to steer the horse and Mama to safety outside, and she was led into our lines beyond the wall.

I re-entered the hall and saw that Aunt Maude was having a fine old time with a slightly wounded Nazi. She waved cheerfully to me and went back to her task of pulling his finger nails off.

I was far too late to save Papa. The bucolic baronet was lying naked in a full bath of vintage port with his arms wrapped around a nubile woman, also starkers. His face was wreathed in a smile so beautiful it seemed a shame to weep over his demise—for dead the old coot was, drowned in his beloved wine. The woman was only very drunk; as I attempted to feel her pulse, she opened one eye and said breathlessly: 'The old bugger got out of the bath three times for a piss.' I left her where she was and crept back to our forces, poised for the final destruction of Hawsbortem Towers.

As the artillery pounded the stately house, I couldn't check the tears that ran down my face. Many memories rambled through my senses, for—despite my peculiar mode of life since childhood—there had been some wonderful moments. Jane sat beside me and she kissed me gently, her caresses awaking all the dormant emotions within me. I was now Sir Peregrine Oswald Potts-Belching, seventh baronet—but at what a price!

'Well done, old chap,' Barton whispered to me during a lull in the onslaught. 'Do you think Hitler is finally laid to rest?'

I shrugged my shoulders wearily. 'I can't see how he could have possibly survived. If the guns didn't pop him off, Aunt Maude must surely have done so.'

Rodney grinned. 'She's a poppet isn't she?'

In response I trembled—poppet indeed! Single-handed, she'd seen about fifty men off. God knows what she would have been capable of when she was a teenager.

The barrage stopped and troops moved into the Towers. It

was all over. Television worldwide reported the end of the Fourth Reich and, all over Britain, Hitler's sympathisers were surrendering to the authorities. There and then, I asked Jane to marry me; and, amid cheers from the men grouped round us, she heartily agreed.

Goodbye the old life, welcome the new.

The Institution,
Miresea-on-Crouch
July 15th

Dear Mr Dawson,

Another long silence from you.

I don't think I can stand it.

The responsibility is too much for me. I can't go on sharing these secrets with you, not after all this time, if there is to be no future for us.

I have shown everything to Chief Inspector Horace Munche, a very nice man whose often given me a cup of tea when one of his constables has found me stuck in the thicket. He says not to worry—but I do. Especially since I met this woman called Ethel Maggs, and she's shown me letters her friend Lily Sidebottom sent her.

(Ethel came into the home for a rest: she kept dreaming she was being chased by a kangaroo.)

Yours, in utter despair,

Amy Pluckett (miss)

Amy Pluckett (Miss)
ps Do you want a Zeppelin heatshield?

From Lily Sidebottom, 1955

Dear Ethel,

Hope you are keeping well in Australia, and thanks for the photographs. Haven't the twins grown? Although we miss you very much, you did the right thing in emigrating. It's bloody awful here in England—I think we were better off when Hitler was in charge. The weather was better then, it's done nothing but rain this spring, and Mother's back is bad again, she's a saint she is. Not much to tell you, it's very dreary here.

Alice Sames got married to a Polish carpenter, I was invited but since my Bert passed away, I don't like going out much. Frankly, I've been very lonely, but I've taken in a lodger and what a nice gentleman he is. He's called Alfred and he's no trouble at all. He sits in his room playing records of marching bands, and he's decorated the entire house for me. He's an elderly man but agile for his age if you know what I mean.

Must go, Fred and Alec are taking me to bingo at the Rialto tonight, Alec wants me to marry him but he's ruptured.

God Bless You and Bill,

Love

Lil

Lil.

Dear Ethel,

Sorry for not having written sooner, it doesn't seem that long since my last letter to you but here we are in August already. Mother's back is worse and Alec is in hospital for a hernia operation (he tried to lift me up at Lent and his truss split). Alfred, my lodger, is a marvellous man, but he won't stop painting the kitchen. It's good of him I know, but he will persist in going over the walls again and again.

He said a funny thing the other night. I said, 'Oh, not painting the pantry again, Alf,' and he said, 'Tthe pantry today, tomorrow the world.' Isn't that odd?

I went in to clean his room—not that it needs it, he's so tidy—and in one of his drawers in the sideboard (you know, the one I got from the Co-op five years ago) well, I found some snaps of his family. A nice lady, somebody called Eva and a man in uniform called Martin. He must have relations on the Continent because he sends food parcels to someone called Rudolph in Berlin. Apparently, from what he's said, this man lives on his own. Shame isn't it?

Billy Forbes' cat was run over last week. Alice left her husband, remember she married a Pole? Anyway she's living over a bakery with a joiner. Mrs Kipps died of jaundice and was cremated. Her husband took it bad and he's never left the pub.

That's all for now, chuck,

Until Next Time, God Bless You and Bill,

Lil

Lil.

Dear Ethel,

Things are not too good, love. That bloody lodger is getting on my nerves. I got home from the chip shop (I'm only there part-time) and I found he'd painted the outside of the house mauve. I started to tell him off and he went wild with rage and pushed me in the living-room. I think he's round the twist. I heard him muttering about people being a pest and prying into his affairs, and my cat went in his room the other day and the next time I saw it, it had been stuffed with cotton wool.

I went to the police but they were unable to help. Frankly, I think Alfred did it, because I've seen him reading books on taxidermists or something like that. I'm going to ask him to leave. He fair gives me the shivers, he does.

Mother's back is playing her up again and her corsets give her a lot of pain. Alice is back with that Polish fellow she married, and he hit the joiner she was living with with a spanner. Alec is in a bad way, they've had to take one of his things down below off, you know what I mean don't you love? The twins are big aren't they? It must be lovely in Australia now in November, here it's bloody awful, raining all the time and meat's gone up.

My lodger is back in his room, I've just seen him dragging something upstairs. That is the last flaming straw Ethel, he's got to go.

Mavis sends her love and told me to tell you the lump's gone.

Until next time, God Bless You and Bill,

Lil

Lil.

Dear Ethel,

Merry Christmas, love . . . I know it's only December the 2nd, but it will be Xmas when you get this short letter. Well, some funny things have happened since I last wrote to you.

That lodger went, thank God. Well, I say gone, he's got to come back for his belongings—but when I told him to hop it, he didn't say a word. He just looked at me, clicked his heels and buggered off.

I'm really glad, because since he's been away, a policeman came round to ask if I'd seen a man, well Ethel he showed me a photo of the man, and do you know who it was? The Polish fellow, Alice's husband, if you can remember—well it was him!

When I told the copper that the Pole had never been in my house, he looked at me strange-like and said that he'd been seen with my lodger in the local pub, and Mrs Crabb (nosey old git) had seen them going into my house one night! She said my lodger seemed to be holding the Polish fellow up.

Fancy that! Well, I gave the copper a piece of my mind I can tell you. I won't have drink in the house.

Alice came round yesterday in a right state, I told her about the policeman coming and she couldn't believe it either. Alec is out of hospital now and he looks all right but his voice is high-pitched. Mavis said the lump's back and mother is dead. I'm going to Charlie and Joan's for Xmas dinner and the weather is bloody awful, raining all the time, I'll bet it's smashing in Australia now. I was sorry to hear about Bill's fall from the kangaroo, hope his broken neck gets better.

Merry Christmas, Love
God Bless You and Bill.

Lil

Lil.

Extract from memo to publisher, dated July 17th

. . . I can't think how I got mixed up in all this. I was doing a show at Billingham Forum when this old copper, Chief Inspector Horace Munche, came up to me and said he'd been told by Amy Pluckett that I knew all about it. He showed me this statement, and what he'd written as the opening chapter of a thriller—but he didn't know what happened next.

What are you going to do with it all? Last time I heard from you, you were punching a calculator. I put the kindest construction I could on your silence and decided it must have knocked you out . . .

Extract from memo from publisher, dated July 19th

. . . who on earth do you think would want to read a yarn like this . . .

'MY HUSBAND and I came from Australia for a month's holiday. We went to see all our old friends despite the weather which has been, I think you'll agree, bloody awful.

'The person I most wanted to visit was my old school friend, Lily Sidebottom, who has always kept in touch over the years; and even the death of her Bert didn't stop her—mind you, her husband had been poorly for years.

'Well, Inspector, we went round to the house (by the way, you can't miss it, it's painted mauve; her lodger did it last year, I think). She wasn't in and a Mrs Crabbe, one of her neighbours, said she hadn't been seen for over six months and nobody knew where she had gone. I was very upset, as you can imagine, and looked everywhere for her, but I had to give up in the end. Bill and I—that's my hubby, he limps now because he fell off the back of a kangaroo during a barbeque—went on with our holiday. Anyway, we came to London to see the sights, hasn't it changed? We did all the usual rounds of sightseeing and finished up at Madame Tussaud's Waxworks, and it was there that I nearly died, because I saw Lily Sidebottom.

'It nearly floored me, I can tell you. We had just walked on from looking at Doctor Crippen, when we came to a group of figures representing the court of Louis the Fourteenth, and there in the middle, large as life—well wax—was Lily! I couldn't get my breath and Bill had to blow down my blouse.

'Inspector, it is—or *was*—Lily Sidebottom. Every detail, every expression was hers. I had to sit down and compose myself and I very nearly swooned, I can tell you. And don't you tell me I imagined it all. That's Lily in there and I demand you do something about it. Here is the last photograph she sent me of herself, judge for yourself Inspector, there is something rum going on and I want to know what it's all about.'

Munche read the statement over again, sighed deeply and rang for his assistant, Sergeant Mole. Munche had only just got rid of Mrs Maggs an hour ago; the damn woman had been close to hysterics and her husband had insisted on calling Munche 'Blue'.

In the five years he had been a policeman, Munche had never come across such a peculiar tale. Still, he was a brilliant officer, the youngest Detective Inspector ever, and to put the woman at rest he had agreed to go to the waxworks and see for himself. He donned his topcoat and hat, picked up the photograph of the missing Lily Sidebottom—who, up to now, nobody had reported missing—and with his sergeant descended the stairs and drove off to Tussaud's.

The usual crowd of tourists was waiting to go in, something that Munche could never understand, because from what he'd seen most of the exhibits looked like James Stewart. They were ushered in on showing their police identifications, and went straight to the man in charge. Puzzled by the whole affair, he instantly put himself at the detective's disposal. Feeling silly, Munche strolled round the exhibition ambling behind the waxworks director who chatted away until they stopped at the group Ethel had mentioned. Munche looked at the photograph, looked at the group and saw . . . Lily Sidebottom. Even to Munche it came as a shock: it was all too life-like, and a chill ran down his back.

The director saw the look on Munche's face, took a glance at the photograph in Munche's hand, and stuttered: 'What in heaven's name . . . that figure wasn't here a month ago, I'll swear to it . . . Somebody has replaced the Contessa Du Barry with that model.'

Turning to his open-mouthed sergeant, Munche said, quite deliberately, 'Phone the yard, Mole, get the lab boys out here and be quick about it.'

Mole trotted off and Munche said to the director, 'You'll have to close for the rest of the day, until we've got to the bottom of this.'

The director nodded and licked his lips. 'Something is wrong here, Inspector.'

Munche looked at him sharply. 'What do you mean by that?' he said. The director pointed to the figure of Lily.

'That is not a waxwork.' He spoke in a trembling whisper.

I NEVER thought life could be so utterly sweet. Being married to Jane was an experience in rapture; she was a constant source of delight and tenderness. We had purchased a small Tudor cottage in the Cotswolds, with roses around the door, and I was in heaven with my lot. Thanks to my part in the downfall of Hitler's punitive Fourth Reich, which had made Great Britain the laughing stock of the world, incidentally, I had become a sort of shop-soiled national hero . . . My articles about the whole affair, plus my inheritance, had assured Jane and me of a comfortable income which allowed us to pursue our interests: she had her watercolours, and I had my music for flute and my poetry.

The only cloud on our happiness was the odd occasion when I was asked to pose in the nude for homosexual magazines, and once I was groped by a gentleman from the Levant. But that side of my life was over; Jane and I had quite normal relations and we hoped soon for a child to seal our joy.

But our serene world was soon to be broken asunder in the shape of Rodney Barton.

How well I recall that morning in late December. Hoarfrost hung festooned from the trees grouped around the cottage; the meadows and heaving hills in the distance were adorned with a mantle of light snow, and the sky was washed with pale pinks and blues. Jane and I sat in companionable silence at the breakfast table, I engrossed in a passage of musical revelation, she with her crossword puzzle, and the pair of us still managing to convey poached egg and slivers of toast into our innards. The tiny kitchen was warm and Oliver, our somewhat tattered cat, purred gently by the stove . . .

At first, we were both so engrossed in our different pursuits, that we failed to respond to the urgent summons of the front door bell. With an effort I mumbled, 'I'll get it, beloved.' My feelings were mixed when the door opened to reveal the long elegant body of Barton—many memories came flooding back, most of them quite ludicrous.

'What ho,' he trilled in his high nasal whinny. 'Sorry to

barge into the old Shangri La and all that, but we do have a bit of a problem.' Jane kissed him warmly and made him a pot of tea, which he sipped ferociously as he talked. 'It all started with what appeared to be a female lunatic from the Antipodes charging into Scotland Yard and claiming that her missing friend was now a waxwork exhibit in jolly old Tussaud's. An investigation proved that the confounded woman was right . . . the thing in the waxworks was not wax, it was a dead woman who'd been stuffed with kapok.'

I was tempted to laugh, but the expression on Barton's face made me desist. He went on. 'When inquiries were mounted, it seemed that the dead woman—a Mrs Lily Sidebottom—prior to her death, had taken in a lodger. From all accounts he was a bit of a mystery; he disappeared from the lodgings of course, and no trace can be found. Before you ask what has all this to do with you—or me, for that matter—one of the late woman's neighbours (a rancid old bag called Mrs Crabbe) was asked to make up an identikit of the features of the missing lodger, and here it is.' With a vague theatrical flourish, he produced the identikit. When I saw it I paled and felt my skin crawling . . . it was so obviously Adolf Hitler.

'Bit of a shaker, isn't it?' stated Barton.

It was a masterpiece of understatement, I thought. It now meant that the threat of an atomic detonation was with us again: one left, but where?

Rodney allowed Jane and me to assimilate the bad news, and went on: 'Three weeks later, it was noticed, in the House of Commons, that the Honourable Member for the constituency that includes the village of Ruff-On-The-Ole, hadn't said a word for hours. Upon inspection, it was found that the man was dead; had been for some time; he had also been stuffed with cotton wool. Then the full impact of the bizarre murders entered a new dimension.'

Barton paused, ground out his cigarette, and resumed. 'Whipsnade Zoo reported that three bears, a mongoose and a puma had all been found stuffed. From Halifax, we heard about the discovery of an entire football team from Barnsley, found on the moors in a coach . . . all stuffed with sawdust. In Scotland, a platoon of Gordon Highlanders were found in a packing case, all dead and stuffed with sheep wool. We believe Hitler is responsible for all these murders. The Department say he must be stopped, otherwise nothing much will move in Britain before long.'

I looked at Barton, and a memory tugged my brain cells. 'I remember once, Hitler said to me that the British race was so slow to rouse into any action, to all intents and purposes they might as well be made of wood,' I said slowly. 'In fact he remarked once, upon seeing a stuffed rabbit in a Weymouth shop, that he admired taxidermists, because they converted mortal flesh into lasting life forms . . . I think Hitler went mad in Hawsbortem Towers and this is the result.'

Rodney nodded in agreement. 'Exactly our thinking, dear boy, and that's where I'm afraid you must come into it again. You were the only one he cared about and, if he sees you, we feel it might draw the madman out into the open. Then we can nail him and find out where the last wretched device is hidden; and defuse it. Your country needs you, Peregrine.'

Jane held me close. 'Rodney's right, darling, you must help to catch him,' she said in her low musical voice. The thought of my beloved Jane, nude with kapok trailing out of her bum, resolved me.

'Whatever you want me to do, I'll do it,' I replied stoutly.

Rodney patted my shoulder and told me the plan. 'We intend to put you on television, in cinema commercials and also in anything which has high ratings appeal. Remember, nobody knows what you look like; even after we put the Fourth Reich to rest and you were acclaimed for your part in it, we never allowed you to be filmed or photographed. It means of course that you will have to play the girl again, but we feel it's the only way to draw the idiot out.'

In my heart of hearts I knew he was right. I'd always managed to turn Adolf on, but dressing up again? I was worried. Would it make me revert to being effeminate? I looked at Jane and knew that it wouldn't. The die was cast. I packed a few things in my case, soundly embraced my Jane amid a flood of tears, and prepared to go with Barton back to London.

Jane waved from our cottage door and the journey to another nightmare began. To make conversation, I asked idly how Aunt Maude was keeping. The effect of my words had a profound impact on Rodney. He braked the car heavily into a lay-by, and put his head in his hands. 'That's the one thing I have kept from you, Perry,' he almost sobbed. 'Aunt Maude is helping Hitler to select his victims. It is she who does the killing, him the stuffing.'

As I sat there aghast, he told me that since the end of the Nazi bid for power, Aunt Maude had been fretful. She'd slit a few throats in Whitechapel. 'We hushed it up, put her in a nice home for genteel ladies but she was pining away for action and she was caught in the nick of time, trying to throttle an Irish navvy,' Barton whispered. 'She escaped from custody and, from all accounts, she's teamed up with Adolf.' I was numb with shock. Hitler I could take, but not an ancient lady assassin. I certainly hadn't banked on that.

We drove in silence the rest of the way to London.

Rodney had arranged for me to stay in a comfortable discreet hotel in Bayswater, and dressmakers were sent round as well as wig-fitters. It was most embarrassing for all concerned, and one chap with a pout touched me up.

Meanwhile, Barton kept me informed about what was going on, and it wasn't very pleasant. Up to now the press had been kept out of it, but before long they would be bound to catch on to the sensational story. Barton told me that a bishop in Ely had been found in the cathedal stuffed with waste paper, three go-go dancers in a Soho club didn't go any more . . . all stuffed. The heavyweight championship of the British Empire had to be postponed when the challenger for the boxing title was found in his changing room stuffed with resin.

Everywhere, Hitler was leaving a trail of destruction and stuffed people—it obviously could not be allowed to continue. The Royal Family, now back in the Palace, were being closely guarded as was the Prime Minister (although many officials firmly believed he'd been born stuffed).

For myself, I was booked for a series of commercials, dressed very much the way it was hoped Hitler would remember me. Within a month I had taken part in a commercial for toilet rolls, another one for corn plasters, and one for an upset stomach. My radiant features were to be seen on city billboards holding a packet of cigars; I played a rival to Bebe Daniels in a television variety show; and one agent tried to get me on his casting couch.

I toured the country in a strip revue called 'Bareway to Stardom' and before long I was in great demand as a stripper. My particular claim to fame was my Dance of the Erotic Banana which seemed to drive the raincoat brigade wild, and I received bunches of flowers every night. Warner Brothers asked me to star in a film about the life of Greta Garbo, and the London Palladium beckoned. Most nights I would phone Jane up and she, dear creature, was a source of help and tips regarding men's attitudes to women, and the best places to buy exotic underwear.

There was still no move from Hitler, however and, indeed, his activities did appear to have slowed down; though one case was reported from Winsford where a bacon smoker was found in a ditch stuffed with ham fat. It was on a Monday night in the Plaza Club, Wigan, that events took a new twist. I was playing to a packed house, dressed in nothing but feathers, waving my banana about to the shouts of, 'Get 'em off!' Security men were posted in the audience, as well as a beefy type in my dressing-room. Everything went well: money was being thrown on to the stage and as I swirled amidst the smoke to the harsh drumming sound from the small band, the men were trying to grab my legs and pull me down. At the conclusion of my act, the noise was deafening and I took three curtain calls and a rude proposition.

I skipped back to my dressing-room, entered it, sat down to remove my eye-lashes and was about to speak to the secret agent behind the door, when I noticed—to my horror—that there was a bale of hay sticking out of his trousers. I went cold. I touched him on the shoulder and he rolled on to the floor . . . He'd been well and truly stuffed.

I was rigid with fear and, when a hand dropped on my nape, I whirled around and there was Adolf—older, greyer but with the same little moustache and dressed in a white smock. One look at his eyes told me that he was completely crackers. Before I could speak, Aunt Maude came tripping out of the wardrobe and warmly kissed me and hugged me. As she did so she whispered lovingly: 'I know that you are a man, but you make him so happy, my dear. He lets me do my own stuffing now.'

Hitler kissed me and said breathlessly, '*Mein* darling, oh my love, I have found you again . . . now we never part, no?' If it had not have been for Aunt Maude, he'd have had me there and then on the sofa, but she tugged his arm impatiently.

'Come Adolf, we've work to do first.' Hitler roared with triumph, and yelled: 'England stuffed today . . . Tomorrow the world.' With that I was bundled out of the window and into a waiting car, and off we sped towards the A1.

It will take many years before I can fully recover from that dreadful journey. On the way to London, those two awesome horrors stuffed a poacher, a petrol pump attendant, two lorry drivers and a pensioner who'd had a drink. Aunt Maude never once drove under a hundred miles an hour, and when chased by a police car, she braked heavily, trotted over to the police officers and strangled them both. On top of all that, Adolf kept trying to take my clothes off and at one point when his hand was up my knicker leg, I had to bash him with a jack handle to discourage the fool.

We reached the outskirts of the city in record time, in fact we'd got there so fast, I complained of weightlessness . . . twice I'd blacked out when my nose began to bleed. Hitler went for a pee in Holland Park, and I took the opportunity of telephoning Rodney Barton. He was delighted with events and I heard him bark out orders for road blocks to be set up around Shepherd's Bush and the Bayswater Road. I gave him the licence number of the lunatic's car and sent Aunt Maude's love to him. Hitler was zipping himself up when I vacated the phone booth and Auntie Maude was changing a tyre.

'The old one was a bit bald, dearie,' she crooned.

This delay suited me and I kept a watchful eye for the arrival of Barton's men. Caught unawares, I was thrown to the ground by Adolf who started kissing me with gusto; we rolled about the grassy verge and the bloody idiot was getting the better of me. I shudder to think what might have happened but for the sound of police cars racing to our position. Hitler sat up, coughed some strands of groundsel from his wet lips, and bundled me into the car. Maude revved the vehicle up and nothing on earth could have matched her speed. We roared past the Shepherd's Bush Common, narrowly avoiding several police cars in the process, and Maude then skidded the car into a narrow alley way that lay at the side of the Shepherd's Bush Empire.

Adolf, Maude and I crept into the stage door of the theatre and, before the stage door keeper could open his mouth, Maude had belted him across the throat with the side of her horny hand. The poor chap went down like a sack of spanners. Music filtered through from the stage area and some pretty chorus girls, waiting to go on, gazed at our weird trio with some justifiable trepidation. I looked back towards the stage door and sighed with relief as the tall figure of Rodney Barton hove into view.

Hitler saw him at the same time and dragged me on to the stage. The audience, or what there was of them (I found out later that business that week had been so bad, somebody had shot a stag in the balcony), started to laugh as the deranged dictator and I stood blinking in the spotlights. Hitler screamed: 'Shut up you pigs' and the audience roared. I glanced down to the orchestra pit and saw that Aunt Maude was busy butchering the band.

Adolf started walking up and down the stage, oblivious to the hordes of policemen hovering in the wings. He sang a German drinking song and the crowd joined in—it was a catchy tune and I couldn't resist warbling a snatch myself. Aunt Maude had finished stuffing the flute player with cotton wool balls, and she accompanied us upon the piano. Hitler, flushed with the applause, broke into 'Lili Marlene' and the whole theatre joined in, including Rodney and his men. 'Take your clothes off, *mein liebe*' shouted Adolf, and I began to do my strip routine . . . It brought the house down. As the last few bars of 'Lili Marlene' died away, Maude grabbed my left hand, Adolf the right one, and we leapt off the stage and down the centre aisle, closely pursued by Barton, policemen, and four theatrical agents waving commission sheets.

Aunt Maude shot a plain-clothes man with a sickening

looking Luger and we bolted into the road where she commandeered a taxi. 'Where are we going?' I panted.

Adolf, his eyes betraying his madness, smiled thinly. 'One bomb I haf left, *ja*? Well, we go now to blow it up.' I paled—even the fact that we were being hotly chased by Barton's men could not reassure me. Down Bayswater Road we raced, round Marble Arch, down Park Lane, hitting a small lorry in the process. Barton's car was a long way behind, and my fears mounted. Maude juddered the car to a halt at the bottom of the Mall and indicated to me that I should leave the vehicle. Adolf helped me out, busy holding an imaginary conversation with Himmler. It was apparent that he was quite bananas—in a strange sort of way I felt rather sorry for the man. Maude bought three hot dogs from a man in a soiled white coat, and then we strolled over into Trafalgar Square. Not many people were about and even the pigeons seemed depressed; I threw one of the birds my hot dog, and it went into a corner and put a wing down its throat.

Hitler marched towards Nelson's Column, and sank to his knees at the base of it. I watched him put a knife-blade into the mortar around one of the stone blocks and, within minutes, he was working the block loose.

Sirens shattered the eardrums as police cars now surrounded the Square. Hitler was oblivious, concentrating his attention on the task of removing the block. Aunt Maude was stuffing a pigeon, and it was fascinating to see her at work. Rodney Barton, gun in hand, shouted to Hitler to surrender, but Adolf took no notice.

I wandered over to the large knot of grim-faced policemen and confronted Barton. 'It's no use, Rodney,' I said. 'He's barmy, but don't try to rush him yet. We still don't know where the bomb is—unless . . .' A terrible knowledge came to me. 'For God's sake get all your men back! I think the bomb is under Nelson's Column!'

Barton went white, and made as to move nearer to Hitler.

Maude stood up. 'Roddy, don't come any nearer! If you do I'll press this switch and we'll all go up.' She waved a small box with wires sticking out of it.

Barton retreated 'Please, Maude, don't let him do this

terrible thing,' he whispered as he backed away.

Aunt Maude smiled warmly. 'Well, it's what he wants to do. And I'm getting on a bit, love, and my legs are playing me up. It will be a nice way to go, really.'

Hitler looked around him vaguely—he didn't seem to see anybody. 'Come, my little one,' he said, beckoning to me.

I shook my head. 'Sorry, Adolf, I cannot—even if we all go up when you detonate the device.'

He put his arm around my shoulder. 'My little petal, this is our escape, don't you see? The bomb will make the statue go up like a rocket, ha ha!'

I started to say something—but what was the use? He was crackers. Roaring with laughter, Adolf started to climb up the column with the help of a coil of rope from Maude's bag. As he banged in iron hooks, Maude followed him gingerly and the two of them slowly crawled up the side of old Nelson. Sharpshooters were poised ready to bring them down but, fearful of what might happen, Barton didn't give the order to order to fire. Instead all units were sent haring away from the scene.

Half an hour later, the Square was deserted; no life stirred within a mile of the place. Fire engines and ambulances stood waiting and troops in protective clothing were sheltering at the end of Whitehall. Through binoculars, I watched Maude and Adolf scale the last few feet of the column. They heaved themselves up on to the ledge next to the old admiral's feet, then sat down and ate some sandwiches and I could see them drinking from a flask.

Suddenly, there was a loud explosion that shook the entire area like an earthquake; all the windows in Whitehall shattered and Big Ben struck fourteen. It was an incredible sight: Nelson's Column rose in a stately fashion from the ground and slowly went into a graceful parabola. Suddenly the whole of London came to life; people poured into the Square to witness the flight of Nelson. Cars were fired into action to track the course of the stone rocket, which was travelling in the direction of Hyde Park. Courting couples lying on the ground in the Park broke off relations as the majestic admiral flew overhead, then dived into the Serpentine in a shower of sparks.

We got to the scene despite the congested roads, and Barton's men plunged into the icy lake to investigate how to retrieve the hissing Column. They found old Adolf dead; he was lying under the head of Nelson, which had come adrift from the torso. Astonishingly, Aunt Maude survived . . . the ancient mass murderess had only four broken ribs, a fractured collar-bone and smashed dentures. She was lifted out of the water and the ambulance took her to hospital—under a heavy guard, I might add.

The result of the affair made Britain once more the laughing stock of the world, and the Isle Of Wight demanded home rule. The Prime Minister resigned and became a shop steward in a foundry, five leading generals were sacked and the Japanese withdrew all their cameras from London stores.

Despite many tempting offers, I didn't return to stripping for a living but, instead, returned to the cottage and my beloved Jane. Let us hope sincerely that the old saw, 'Time is a great healer', will apply and that soon we can all forget the ghastly chain of events that manacled us all in its lunacy . . .

. . . It doesn't seem nearly three years since Hitler met his end in Hyde Park. Like everything else, the whole affair was a nine-day wonder, and it soon left the national newspaper headlines to make way for Hollywood scandals and charges of bribery in badminton. Aunt Maude was found insane and sent off to a well-guarded mental institution, where she managed—in the space of three months—to stuff the matron with brown paper and a pregnant cat with olives.

For myself, marriage began to pall. I discovered, to my chagrin, that Jane was becoming a nagger: night after night she ranted and cursed, and sometimes she would physically abuse me. She had changed since the birth of our daughter, Effie—a strange baby with a cleft chin and a faint beard.

Frankly, it drove me wild; and I would sit for hours in the meadow, playing a lament on my flute, and longing for the days spent in tranquillity at Hawsbortem Towers. I went to visit Aunt Maude last spring but, as she tried to spear me with a curtain rod, I haven't been since. Rodney Barton was retired early and he was last heard of running a brothel in Dorking.

Time was hanging heavy on my hands at the cottage earlier this year, and so I tried my hand at the art of the taxidermist. I had never forgotten Maude's skill at stuffing the pigeon in Trafalgar Square, and I studied the subject intensely. Within a short time I had stuffed a vole, a squirrel, and a magpie. I was most pleased with my handiwork, but when I displayed them to Jane, she hit me with a brass plaque and threw my creations into a septic tank.

That was in May of this year, but Jane doesn't nag any more . . . oh no. She went too far one night and now she just sits in a chair in the kitchen. I did a good job on her, I must say; she's stuffed with the finest sawdust and kapok money could purchase, oh yes. The baby is getting on my nerves, it won't be long before she joins her mummy.

I begin to see the wisdom of this . . . imagine a world of stuffed people, no more the rantings of politicians, no pop music, women who now only listen . . . Ah, Aunt Maude, you've certainly started something.

Postscript

THAT WAS it. I gave all the material for 'Hitler Was My Mother-In-Law' to the publisher, and had no more letters from Amy Pluckett that year. Not even a Christmas card. Then, one morning early the following May, I received a telephone call from the Institution at Miresea-on-Crouch, asking me to pay a visit to see the doctor in charge. By the timbre of the voice at the other end of the line, I sensed an urgency in the appeal, and so that very day, quite intrigued, I drove down the motorway, and to my appointment in Miresea.

It was, I recall, a nice day—a balmy day indeed; the trees were fully clothed and the rolling hills were ablaze with colour, and as I dipped down into the small resort of Miresea the sea glistened like a freshly-polished emerald. Miresea isn't a well-known resort; in fact, during the war, it's where they stored barbed wire and tank grease. There is a jetty and, on Friday nights, a little Bulgarian band play selections from the

FORMULA 1

Imodium*
First and foremost in diarrhoea

This is your entry number
Please retain this card

`0337`

Imodium

control diarrhoea in 1 hour

FAST AND EASY

Rapid action Ref: [1]

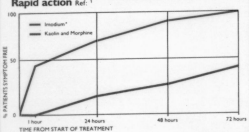

— Imodium*
— Kaolin and Morphine

% PATIENTS SYMPTOM FREE

100

50

0

1 hour · 24 hours · 48 hours · 72 hours

TIME FROM START OF TREATMENT

Convenient dosage

Average quantity of medication required to control diarrhoea

Kaolin and Morphine: 22 × 5 ml spoonfuls

Imodium: 4 capsules

Ref: I. G. I. John MB BS, The Practitioner,
1311, 219, 1977 *Trademark JPL/604/84

picked up a poker and crept to the door and asked who it was. A voice replied, "It's Harold, Auntie. For God's sake open the damn door." Harold it was, shaking like a leaf and looking very, very peaky. I made him a strong cup of coffee and after he'd drank it he told me a bizzare story and it concerns Aunt Maude.'

My mind reeled. Aunt Maude was the elderly looney who had committed all the murders in Hawsbortem Towers, the architect of Peregrine Potts-Belching's ordeal in *Hitler Was My Mother-In-Law.*

'Surely not,' I gasped. 'She was locked up, wasn't she?'

Miss Pluckett gazed at me. 'She was. And she behaved very well. So, in 1973, they let her out—she seemed to be a sweet old lady who wouldn't hurt a fly. Then, two years later, ten old men were strangled and thrown into the Thames by the Mad Butcher Of Acton. You must remember the case. He went crazy filling in a VAT form and killed his grandmother with a sliver of frozen of bacon.' I did recall the trial, which had caused quite a stir and been followed by a slump in meat prices. Had Maude killed for a sirloin?

Miss Pluckett continued. 'Harold was concerned because he firmly believes that his agent is no other than Aunt Maude herself.'

This was too much for me to grasp, and I said as much to Amy Pluckett. She, in return, sighed deeply, and told me the sorry tale that I am putting down for your appraisal. If it's true, then may God help us all; if not, then I too will be shortly ensconced in the Institution for even listening to it.

I have transcribed Amy Pluckett's story in the first person, as if Happy Daze was actually writing it. That way, the full impact of the events hits you with its incredible pattern. Here it is, then:

Happy Daze, and Hollywood

The Testament of Happy Daze . . .

I SAT IN the dusty cubicle that passed as a dressing-room, and
waited for the police to clear the crowd outside who were
trying to break the door down.

I was very close to tears as I sat there on the wooden box
that the club secretary kept the bingo tickets in, and I
clutched my doll, Pepe, in dread as the mob bayed for my
blood. Oddly enough, the night had started off fairly well at
the Mansfield Glue Workers' Social Club. The place was
packed and the audience gave the stripper, Toots La Verne, a
standing ovation when her knickers fell off. They seemed in a
good mood, and when the compère announced my name, I
received a warm hand, despite the fact that last time I had
played the club, a large man had shoved my head in a
bucket. On I dashed to the podium and went into my act
with Pepe, my little Mexican doll:

Me: 'Hello, what's your name?'
Pepe: 'Pepe'
Me: 'Pee Pee?'
Pepe: 'No thanks, I've just been.'
Pepe: 'I have a dog with no nose.'
Me: 'How does it smell?'
Pepe: 'Bloody awful, mate.'
Me: 'You shouldn't swear in front of an audience.'
Pepe: 'No, with this lot you should swear at 'em.'

Not one person present had laughed from the moment I'd
begun and at least three people had drunk up and gone,
always a bad sign. I tried some more patter, which instantly
died on the spot, and then someone threw an empty brown
ale bottle at me. It hit Pepe, and his arm dropped off. That
got a laugh, of course, but I was outraged—and I threw the

bottle back. It unfortunately struck a pregnant lady on the forehead, and she went down like a felled bullock . . . That did it. As one, the uncultured clay rose and it was an hour before the incensed throng dispersed, and I was able to leave. Moodily, I drove through the dreary damp streets of Mansfield, and made my way to London. As the ribbon of motorway yawned before me, not for the first time did I ponder on the drama of my chequered career . . .

My parents had been in show business for years. They did a duet together, singing, as they put it, 'Songs From The Shows.' They had been billed as the 'Aristocrats Of Melody,' and they were regarded as the worst act in entertainment. Mother's voice was similar to a duck breaking wind, and dad's bronchial baritone was like a grampus surfacing in the North Sea.

Season after season they played resorts like Clacton, Morecambe, Cromer, always at the foot of the bill, and it finally took its toll. My father was found wandering in Tring wearing suspenders and a bra, and shouting, 'Delfont is a pouffe.' He was put under close observation and when released, he hung himself in a garden gnome factory in Wiltshire. My mother carried on as a stag stripper; she wanted to be another Gypsy Rose Lee. The trouble was that when she took her clothes off she looked more like Christopher Lee. Eventually she retired and opened a theatrical boarding house in Camden Town, and that's where I grew up, visited occasionally by my eccentric Aunt Amy.

It was a strange environment for a growing lad, this place full of jugglers and comics, singers and actors, none of whom ever made anything of themselves. Mother took up with a tap-dancer who had angina, and she lost interest in me, so really it was the theatricals themselves who taught me about life. I found that show business was wayward and sometimes cruel, but I'd never known anything else so it was natural, I suppose, that I should gravitate to it in later years.

When I reached my late teens, I was taught the art of ventriloquism by a seedy individual who rejoiced in the name of 'The Great Marvo'. (His real name was Bert Potts and he'd lost a foot on the Somme.) From Max Batty, a comedian from Swansea, I learnt about comedy and timing; I should not have heeded his advice, because it turned out that he was the only comedian in history who had been paid off from a charity show. But in those days I didn't know any better, and spent hours in my room practising what they had imparted to me.

One Christmas, mother threw a party for her guests and I was asked to perform for them . . . I did, and mumsie cried and cried in to her beer. From that moment on, she was quite determined that I should be a star. She got the Great Marvo to make me my doll, which I called 'Pepe' and she fixed me up with an interview with the same agent who had managed her and dad. He was a short, bald man called Norbert Murray, with an office in a back street in Soho, and now had only one act—an Indian couple who had a goose that could tell the time.

I auditioned for him, and he fell asleep. I was about to leave in high dudgeon, when he roused himself and informed me, that, because of his affection for my parents, he would give me a chance at a club known as the Commodore. It sounded nice, but when I got there it looked like a well-upholstered potting shed. Thick smoke hung everywhere, the lighting was terrible and, in corners, couples were fornicating on the tables. I did my act and nobody listened; though the silence was so intense that the mere shifting of a cashew nut from one molar to another reverberated like a musket volley. The manager wouldn't pay me and a waiter picked my pocket—that was my introduction to show business.

It was like that for the next two years. After one débâcle in Leeds the kindly club owner sent a priest round to see if he could help me find my way in life. When I played a venue in Glasgow, a retired ghillie tried to push Pepe down my throat. Manchester wasn't kind to me at all. There, in a huge public house that did nightly variety, a disturbed dwarf attempted to set fire to my shirt; I got away in an ambulance.

Finally, I decided that I'd had enough of show business—and when I told mother this, she threw me out of our boarding house. I had one last date in my engagement book, a Derby and Joan club in Watford. Little did I know what I was letting myself in for.

It didn't start off too badly—most of the audience were deaf, and the others dozed off. The superintendent paid me my money, and he took me into his office for a drink before I left. As we sat there, I remarked on the number of stuffed birds he had on his desk. He smiled.

'One of our old ladies has a passion for taxidermy. She isn't all there, I think, but harmless enough.' I shook his hand, picked up the case containing Pepe, and made to go. Just then, a tiny, very old, apple-cheeked, lavender-smelling lady came into the office. Her face was the colour of an autumn sky and her smile was a warm glow. The superintendent put his arm around her shoulder and brought her towards me. 'This is Miss Fox and she is the lady who stuffed these birds for me.' I kissed the delightful lady on her cheek, and she simpered.

'Oh, I did enjoy your act,' she said sincerely. 'You should be on the television, young man.' I basked in her admiration. She went on, 'You may think I'm a silly old woman, but I could help you get on. After all, you do deserve it.'

To this day I don't know why I did, but I gave her my agent's telephone number and my home address—a cold water flat in Notting Hill Gate. I then left and forgot all about it.

I couldn't get a job anywhere, and I tried, I really tried. If it hadn't have been for mum's tap-dancer who sent me the odd bob or two, and Nancy, I would have starved. Oh, I must explain about Nancy—she's a girl I share the flat with. She's a plain sort of person who whips a varied assortment of men for a living. We don't sleep together; she'd have me, I know, but the sight of bull whips and leg irons and masks in the closet puts me off. I confess that I have often put a tumbler to the wall of the adjoining bedroom and listened to the antics she gets up to . . . One night a lapsed Methodist kept asking her to spank him and put oranges in his vest—God knows what a thrill that brings, but it cost him fifty quid. Once I peeped through her bedroom keyhole and saw her dressed as an archbishop, hitting a nude man on the thigh with a German sausage. He was obviously enjoying it and the climax was when he threw up in his sock. To each his own say I, and Nancy makes sure I always have a few pence in my pocket; in return I place ads in the newsagent's for her.

I returned to the flat one late afternoon after a fruitless search for employment, and found a note on the table from Nancy, asking me to ring my agent urgently. I hadn't told Murray that I was giving the business up and, although he'd despaired of me, it seemed I was still on his books. I rang him straight away. What had I got to lose?

His voice sounded strained. 'Hello, Happy, have you seen tonight's paper? The early edition?' he asked hoarsely. I replied in the negative. 'It's the darnedest thing. Ray Allen, the vent, has been found dead . . . I don't know how to put this, but he's been emptied and stuffed with kapok.' I was thunderstruck. Ray Allen, with his Lord Charles, was to my mind one of the best ventriloquists in the world.

'Who could have done such a thing? Have they caught the person who did it?' I gasped.

Murray told me the full story. Ray Allen had been seen leaving home for a date in the Midlands. He had signed some autographs at a service station on the M1, and been found on the hard shoulder several miles further on, still sitting in his car, stuffed. The police were baffled by it but were checking on any recent escapes from mental homes.

'The queer thing is, Happy, I had done a deal on a split commission basis for Ray Allen to play a date tonight in Nottingham. When I saw the paper I rang the club to cancel it, but they told me somebody had recommended you instead. And they've agreed to pay you the same money that they were going to pay Ray Allen!'

Money, that magic word . . . I was off to Nottingham like a shot.

The club was marvellous, carpeted and luxurious, and I did my act:

Me: 'Well Pepe, what do you think of Nottingham?'
Pepe: 'I don't know, I've never put knots in ham.'
Me: 'Robin Hood lived here and Maid Marion.'
Pepe: 'Everybody in Sherwood Forest made Marion.'
Me: 'King John lost his jewels in the Wash.'
Pepe: 'Serves him right for using a laundrette.'

Just then, a man in the audience shouted, 'What a rotten

act! You can see his mouth move! Get off, bloody awful.'

That started it. People stood up, hurling abuse at me, and the rest of my performance was drowned out by the noise. The compère hurriedly came on stage and started to sing 'The Lady Is A Tramp', while two club bouncers hustled me off the podium and out into the wings. The manager sent for me and gave me half my agreed fee, saying that if I ever entered his premises again, he would shove Pepe up my arse and break my collar-bone.

When I got back to London I felt so dreadful that I knocked on Nancy's bedroom door—I needed someone to unburden my troubles to. She opened the door dressed as Atilla The Hun, carrying a clergyman in her arms. He was nude apart from his dog collar and gaiters, and he was smeared in potted meat. She listened to my plea for a hearing, nodded, and dumped the clergyman on to the bed with a promise to come back to him soon.

I told here what had transpired at the club in Nottingham and she was most sympathetic. After she left the room to see to her client, I made my mind up to quit show business for all time.

IT WAS the shrill note of the telephone which brought me to the surface of consciousness. After my chat with Nancy the night before, I had gone to bed with a bottle of gin and guzzled the entire contents in a fit of despair. I picked up the receiver and grunted, and the voice of my agent grated my eardrum: 'Happy? Is that you?'

I shifted my inert frame into a more comfortable posture, and said somewhat acidly, 'No, It's Robert Redford, and I'm just about to mount Jane Fonda.'

'Listen, you idiot. God only knows what is going on, but last night Max Bygraves was found in his dressing-room at Thames Television—and he had been stuffed with river sand.'

Instantly I was alert. Murray poured out the full horrific story as with trembling fingers I lit a Woodbine butt. Max had been rehearsing all day for his new show, when a lightning strike of technicians had halted taping. Max had gone into his dressing-room to count his money; an hour later, a callboy had found him in his dressing-gown, dead and stuffed to his gills with sand. The police were unable to keep the story out of the Press, and the whole country rocked with horror while the records of 'Singalonga Max' were poised to shoot up in the charts.

Suddenly, over the phone, I heard my agent say, 'Who's that?' I presumed that somebody was knocking at his office door, and I heard Murray shout, 'Wait a minute please,' then he came back to me.

'Happy, I don't know what's going on, but I had a strange letter the other day about you. Jesus, it put the wind up me! I must see you . . . I told you to wait . . . what the hell is this . . . Hey!'

The telephone went dead. I sat there cradling the instrument and a digit of fear crawled up my spine. I dressed hurriedly and left the flat to go to Murray's office. My car wouldn't start, and I sat there fuming against the salesman who had sold me the car, telling me I'd get a lot of pleasure out of it. He was right—it was a pleasure to get out of it. The car was an automatic; in heavy traffic, it stopped automatically. It had leaf springs and they fell off in autumn. I don't know who'd owned the car before me, but the log book was in Latin.

Just then, Nancy came out of the decaying block which houses our flat. She tutted sympathetically, and gave me a lift in her new Porsche. The radio was on and the news was all about Max Bygraves. The latest bulletin said that both he and Ray Allen were now standing up in a warehouse in Ealing. Several suspects had been questioned by the police, including Des O'Connor and a retired arsonist. The police admitted that there was a maniac at large and that at present they had no clues to follow up.

Nancy pulled up outside my agent's office, and nervously I asked her to come with me to see Murray . . . I don't know what prompted me to ask her to be my companion, but that digit of fear was now parting my hair.

We walked down the musty corridor to the accompaniment of music from dance studios that escorted the walk to Murray's agency; his office door was wide open. My heart was beating furiously as we approached his untidy sanctum: there was no sign of his secretary and that was a bad omen, because Norbert Murray, as well as using her as a mistress, relied on her for everything.

Murray was sitting in his big leather chair, a chair so old that it had probably carried Hannibal across the Alps. He was facing the window which overlooked a sex shop opposite. Nancy went to him first, and swivelled the chair round.

Murray was dead as mutton and he had lengths of straw hanging out of his ears . . . He'd been well stuffed. I nearly fainted and Nancy looked quite pale.

In the office stood a large cabinet and I knew what I would find inside. I opened it gingerly, and saw the secretary on her knees, nude and with cotton wool protruding from her mouth and rectum.

By now I was a quivering mass—Nancy took charge and phoned the police who arrived, sirens blaring, within a few minutes. A dapper police surgeon examined the corpses and said briskly to the senior man, Chief Inspector Horace Munche, 'Sliced down the middle, innards removed, stuffed with different materials and sewn up again. Nice stitching I must say; neat and good quality twine used. Seems as though cause of death is the same as in the other cases—hit with a blunt instrument.'

The inspector nodded and eyed me suspiciously. Nancy and I told him everything we knew, including the telephone call that Murray had made to me. He merely grunted and loftily informed us both not to leave town.

The bodies were removed in a plain furniture van and taken to the warehouse in Ealing to join the others, and Nancy and I went home. I would have prefered to go for a drink, but she had to get back to see a draughtsman who liked to be tickled with emu feathers. Back in our flat, I sat and tried to make sense of things, but my mind would not function. I knew that I was involved in some way but for the life of me I couldn't figure it out. It was difficult to concentrate, what with the draughtsman next door running about laughing and Nancy playing a bugle, and my nerves jangled even more when the telephone rang.

'Hello? Happy Daze?' a voice said. I'd heard the voice before, a low elderly sort of voice, a woman's . . . but I couldn't place it. 'I want you to see Mr Dennis Belfont. I've made an appointment for you tomorrow morning at eleven thirty, be a good lad and be on time . . . I told you I could help your career, and I am doing just that. You see, Dennis Belfont is a very good friend of mine, and I believe he is a wonderful theatrical agent. Good luck, you nice boy!' The penny dropped. It was the old lady that I'd spoken to at the Derby and Joan club in Watford.

How nice of her, I thought at the time . . . Well, here we go again, Daze. It would be worth keeping the appointment because Belfont was one of the best agents in the business; with that happy thought I knocked on Nancy's bedroom door to tell her the news. She opened it, looking startling in her red frogman's outfit and flippers, and I glimpsed a thin man dressed in a mauve frock bending over a chair, chained by his wrists to a labrador pup. Nancy beamed when I told her the news, and even her client shouted, 'Bravo!'

I almost skipped back to my room and sat down with hope springing in my soul. I switched the television on; there was a film on, a Western so old that Gabby Hayes got the girl and the Indians attacking the fort meant it. Abruptly the screen went blank, and on came a news flash. The newsreader, Kenneth Kendall, looked very solemn as he spoke:

'Late this afternoon, comedian Bob Monkhouse was found at home with his head in a jar of dimple cream. It appears he was another victim of the murderer who stuffs his prey with a variety of materials. In Mr Monkhouse's case, the police surgeon said that the comedian had been stuffed with pulped scripts after death. This came as somewhat of a shock to his show-business friends who said Monkhouse never had much of a script. Police are continuing their search for the maniac and warn all householders to bolt their doors before retiring for the night.'

The film came back on and Randolph Scott sneered at me.

The next day, promptly at 11.30 I sat in the well-appointed office of Mr Dennis Belfont who didn't look at all easy about meeting me. We shook hands and he tried to muster a smile;

it turned out a sort of gastric grimace. 'Er, yes . . . Happy Daze. Well, it seems that some people think very highly of you . . . Highly . . . Yes.' He seemed to have difficulty in finding words to say. I decided to take the bull by the horns.

'Mr Belfont, sir,' I said quietly. 'Frankly, I fail to understand why you of all people should be taking such an interest in me. I'm a third-rate performer and I know it. With my act, sir, I should be rapping on a cathedral portal and begging for sanctuary. I came here today, because a kind old lady said she knew you very well . . . What's the matter?' Belfont had slumped, with his head in his arms, and was sobbing his heart out like a bride who's been left at the altar. I thought he'd never stop.

I lent him my handkerchief and he blew his nose hugely upon the soiled fabric. 'I'm sorry, Daze old chap . . . Don't know what came over me.' He stopped talking and bit his lip.

'Something is wrong, Mr Belfont, very wrong, and I feel that I am in some way connected with it all,' I told him.

Belfont stared at me. 'How long have you known the old lady who calls herself Miss Fox?' he whispered.

'I met her at a Derby and Joan club when I did a concert for the old folks. Just who is she?' I asked him. He didn't reply at once, and when he finally did it was with enormous difficulty . . .

'I haven't always been a theatrical agent,' he said. 'I used to work for the government, and more than twenty-five years ago I was involved in a most incredible business at Hawsbortem Towers, the home of the Potts-Belching family. Suffice to say, it was the trickiest situation that I have ever found myself in, and I've been in a few. I retired early, and for some years ran a house of . . . entertainment in Dorking. Then in 1973 I changed my name from Barton to Belfont, and entered showbiz . . .' He broke off as the telephone rang, excused himself to me and picked up the receiver. I watched the blood drain from his face.

'Oh no! My God, this can't be true!' He looked at me, and his eyes were pits of horror. 'Mr Daze, forgive me, but they have found the entire touring company of the Black and

White Minstrel Show dead and stuffed with sawdust in a permissive sauna bath in Reading.' He put the instrument down and buried his head yet again in his hands.

I didn't know what to do but simply sat there and ran an exploratory tongue over my dry lips. I was about to speak when the phone rang again. Belfont appeared to know who the call was from; his features became ashen and his hands trembled like aspen leaves. 'Yes, yes, I've heard the news. Please—no more, I'll do as you say.' He stared at me in a strange fashion, and dumbly held out a contract in my direction.

I took it and read that I, Happy Daze, would be the star of a new television series called 'The Daze Of Variety.' Thunderstruck, I felt the digits of fear creep once again up the back of my shirt.

Dennis Belfont (once Rodney Barton) was a broken man; it was obviously useless trying to pump him for the information that I desperately needed . . . Oh yes, something was definitely wrong in the state of Denmark, and I was bang in the middle of it. As I left the office I heard Belfont muttering a name over and over again—it was hard to catch what he was saying but it sounded like 'Maude, Aunt Maude.'

My début on television was a disaster on the lines of the sinking of the *Titanic*. I fluffed my script, knocked a microphone over, accidentally pulled a plug out, and the studio audience fell about with laughter—the deluded fools thought it was part of the programme. The following day, a newspaper critic wrote in his column that I was a disgrace to the medium; the next night, around 6 p.m., he was discovered in bed stuffed with dried watercress. The warehouse in Ealing was getting pretty full by now: Dave Allen was there, stuffed with kapok and tobacco dust; so was Ken Dodd, stuffed with old money and dandruff; Hughie Green was propped up against a wall, well and truly bunged up with pieces of a shag pile carpet. I was now under the watchful eye of the European police forces.

Over and over again, I was interrogated; and time and

time again, they had to let me go. I was getting plenty of work now simply because there was hardly any pro performers left that moved. Esther Rantzen was found heavily stuffed with dental paste in Dulwich; nobody knew where the assassin would strike next. Jimmy Tarbuck was found on the sixteenth green of a golf course: he'd been stuffed with finely-ground golf balls and mole droppings. All this was too much for a lot of artistes, and they quit the business to save their necks: Bruce Forsythe opened a gent's outfitter's in Hamburg; Des O'Connor took a job towing caravans to Devon, and his records were bought by hospitals and used for putting patients to sleep.

I found that people were terrified of me, and when Tommy Cooper was discovered standing at a bar, stuffed with powdered wine-bottle corks, it was too much for Paul Daniels, who ran away and became a grocer in the Ardennes. Larry Grayson gave it all up and went as a trainer with a rugby team, and was deliriously happy; Morecambe and Wise opened their own bank.

Inspector Horace Munche of the Yard went with me to the mental home at Miresea-On-Crouch. We were acting now on information gleaned from my aunt, Amy Pluckett, who had once been an inmate there, when she was going through her brace and bit period. We were given permission to see Peregrine Potts-Belching, and it wasn't long before he was screaming blue murder about Auntie Maude. The pieces of the jigsaw came together at last.

It was she indeed who was doing the stuffing—I should have remembered the birds in the superintendent's office at the Derby and Joan club . . . Miss Fox, alias Aunt Maude, had committed wholesale slaughter so that I would get on television.

The Les Dawson Report

MISS AMY PLUCKETT, Happy Daze and I met secretly at the home. Daze was a frightened man—and I didn't blame him. Since the identity of the mass killer had been broadcast,

Maude had phoned Happy up and told him that she was very disappointed with him. Which meant that, if the old looney got her hands on him, he'd finish up in the warehouse. The next day he got a letter from her asking for commission.

Frankly, the whole affair was mystifying to me. Of course I'd read all about entertainers being killed and stuffed, but I'd put it down to an attack of good taste by the public. Now the hunt was on for Aunt Maude—but where was she? In one week she was reported to have been spotted in Wales, Tenerife, Oslo and Oldham. The Press was censored in order to halt the growing panic, because, by now, Maude was stuffing anybody she could lay her hands on. A charabanc of pensioners, all stuffed with lavender, was found in Clacton. In the Tower of London, an American lady from Ohio had to be given on-the-spot medical help when she patted a Beefeater on the back and he fell over: he'd been rammed full of Army blanco. Nothing moved at all in Regent's Park Zoo, and a fruit bat was found being used by a model as an umbrella. Tourist trade dropped right off when a Japanese Origami expert was found stuffed with patna rice in Selfridge's. Maude had obviously gone bananas, and she had to be captured.

As I saw it, Happy Daze would have to be the bait. The police agreed with me, their decision shaped by the fact of two constables in Watford discovered stuffed with charge sheets. Daze wasn't too enraptured by the idea, but he had no choice in the matter; and, with the help of BBC Outside Broadcasts, a trap was laid for the Mad Aunt.

The plan was a simple one. Billy Cotton, the least harmless of all BBC overseers, gave the go-ahead for a series of concerts—featuring Happy Daze—to be recorded in municipal parks all over the country. It was hoped that this would draw Aunt Maude into the open—something had to be done, and quickly. A Jesuit on holiday in the Cotswolds bought a garden pixie because it looked like Ronnie Corbett—when he got it back to Liverpool, he realised with horror that it was Ronnie Corbett, who had been stuffed with horse hair and shavings and pebble-dashed. Ronnie Barker went into exile in Corfu, and Dame Flora Robson appealed for Maude to join Equity.

There was no longer any room left in the warehouse in Ealing, and quite a few of the stuffed theatrical victims were sent to Madame Tussaud's and put on display in an effort to keep the rates down.

Happy Daze was virtually the only television personality left now, and he was on the box every night. Monday he was cajoled into reading the nine o'clock News after Robin Day was found stuffed with steamed lentils in Chiswick; Tuesday he played three parts in 'Crossroads' when a trio of the regular members of the soap opera were discovered in a trunk in the motel; Wednesday in 'Coronation Street' he portrayed the licensee of the Rover's Return after the actress who normally played the role was found stripped and crammed with bacon-flavoured potato crisps.

A state of emergency was declared by the Queen after Friday found that most of the back bench of the Government were lined up in Whitehall, well and truly embalmed with feathers. Russia withdrew her embassy staff, and broke off diplomatic relations. President Reagan condemned Britain's secret weapon, scorning our pleas that one old maniac was responsible for it all, and took his cruise missiles away and bunged them in the Isle Of Man. The Prime Minister broadcast to the nation, and tried to appeal for calmness, but the population was jittery and law and order was beginning to break down.

Wearily, I stumbled into a taxi in Regent Street, and then stumbled out again, because Maude had got to the driver first and he was sitting at the wheel with straw pouring out of his ears and chest. I had been summoned to an emergency meeting in Whitehall, where plans had been drawn up first of all to find Aunt Maude, and then detonate a small bomb over her. France had denounced Great Britain and had accused us of attempting to overthrow the Common Market; and, in retaliation, they had decided not to import our carrots.

I was met in the War Office by General Hagbottle, and he fixed me with an icy glare. 'Look here, my good man, something has got to be done about this infernal woman.

She's ruining the blasted country, and Boycott hasn't scored in the Test yet.'

I was mortified. 'Good heavens, sir,' I expostulated, 'don't tell me she's stuffed Boycott as well?' The General scratched his seat with a fly swat, and said impatiently, 'God's blood, no, you ass, Boycott's playing his usual game. Now see here, Billy Cotton has got all his cameras and things ready in Hyde Park for tonight's concert featuring this Happy Daze johnny. It's your job to make damn sure he gets there, what?'

I nodded and he grunted, finished off his Planter's Punch, and left for Lord's.

Hyde Park was lit ready for the concert, and sections of the SAS were in position. Happy Daze was surrounded by bodyguards and was quite safe for the time being. I strolled around, feeling secure in the presence of the Marines and other fighting units, and I didn't believe for one moment that Aunt Maude would show up. There are almost a carnival atmosphere in the air: vendors selling hot dogs and Cornish pasties, bookmakers giving odds on the capture of Aunt Maude, a punk rock band playing in a tree house, and a troupe of Morris Dancers from Ormskirk being mugged in a lavatory.

I espied General Hagbottle sitting upright against a diseased elm, and squatted next to him for a reflective smoke. I chatted on for about a minute or two then the chilled digits of fear once more inched across my spinal column. General Hagbottle was dead . . . and he had been stuffed with curry powder and bay leaves. He had a sort of chagrined look on his bucolic face, and in his hand he held a cricket stump.

My heart began to beat wildly, and I was about to flee like a startled wombat, when a cooing sort of voice stopped me in my tracks. 'What a lovely night, is it not? All the young people enjoying themselves. Ah, sweet bird of youth, how swiftly it flies away.'

I turned round, shaking. There, behind me, sitting on a bench and knitting, was Aunt Maude. Suddenly my fears drained away. It was inconceivable, that this small, sparrow-like old lady could have been responsible for the wave of peculiar murders. Her lined countenance was the very epitome of compassion and serenity. Her delicate hands fluttering about her knitting needles were but withered leaves, not the mandibles of assassination; they were fronds to stroke the fevered brow of a sick child, or to calm the nerves of a loved one. Her grey curls peeped out from under a delightful little fluffy hat, and the faint wind blew the straggled ends of her hair into ringlets around her pink ears. Her eyes were tiny lances of blue; lagoons of wisdom set in age-shadowed pits, and her pert nose had a hint of impertinence in its contour. Her lips were dried and pursed and her chin had small warts with bristles on. Aunt Maude wore a woollen twinset, brown and beige; a string of pearls as decoration round the neckline; thick lisle stockings, sensible brogues and, as protection from the cold night air, she had a short fur coat draped around her stooped shoulders. She looked at the body of General Hagbottle.

'Such a distinguished man, don't you think?' she murmured as the knitting needles clicked. 'It's a shame when you think nice men like him will die one day. That's why I took all the things out of his tummy and filled him up with lovely spices so that he will be with us for ever and ever.'

With those words, my fear returned. She was cracked, all right, and I was too close for comfort. Out of the corner of my eye, I saw two SAS men approaching. Getting to my feet, I casually said to Maude, 'It's a wonderful thing you did for the old general. I'd like to introduce you to two of my best friends; you'll like them, they're very nice.'

Aunt Maude shyly glanced at me, patted her hair and replied, 'I'd love to meet them, do I look all right?'

On impulse, feeling rather like a Judas, I kissed her gently on the cheek; though I knew that I might have put a stop to her antics, nevertheless I had tears of regret in my eyes as I said to her meaningly, 'You look so lovely my dear, they'll throw themselves at your feet.'

She simpered slightly and resumed her knitting; I motioned the SAS men to come over. 'That is Aunt Maude, chaps. Don't be fooled by her appearance, she's the one. Do be careful.' One of them nodded, and slipped the safety catch off his machine pistol.

They guided Aunt Maude towards a tent, which I knew was full of security men, and I went off to tell Miss Pluckett's nephew, the celebrated Happy Daze, that all was well.

The concert went off as scheduled, and Happy did all right because only a handful of us knew that Aunt Maude had been taken into custody. Everybody was so tense that they took little notice of Happy Daze, being more intent on peering for a glimpse of the dreaded Aunt. I think Happy did a lot for people's morale that night—most of the audience were asleep before he'd finished, and the rest did them good. The Prime Minister congratulated me most profusely on being responsible for the aprehension of Aunt Maude, and he promised me a first edition of Wedgwood Benn's *Good Humour Book*.

Nobody gave a hang now for Happy Daze—in fact Billy Cotton kicked him heavily in the groin, and a Siamese cat peed up his arm. I escorted the Prime Minister over to the rostrum where he was about to tell the country—indeed, the world—that Maude had been copped. He insisted that I, a lowly wordsmith, should stand and rub shoulders with him during the broadcast; and, for good measure, he groped my bum. This didn't shock me one iota; he was often seen in East End urinals with a masked cadet and an ostrich. He cleared his throat, and then boomed forth:

'Tonight, the maniac who has virtually brought this great country of ours to a halt, who has betrayed the code of conduct that this government helped to restore after the flagrant abuses that the other party heaped upon our luckless heads, whose idiotic policies cost us dearly in terms of full employment and friendship with the Isle of Wight . . .'

On and on the windbag droned, all thought of Maude gone as he ground out his election manifesto instead. Suddenly, I saw Nancy looming towards me, attired as a nun and carrying a sandbag. 'Happy Daze said I'd find you here. You'd better come quickly, we've got more trouble.' I vacated the podium as the Prime Minister bawled ever on.

Nancy fascinated me; I recognised her from Happy's description, and of course the strange costume helped to cement the identification. She took me to the tent where I'd seen the SAS men lead Auntie Maude. We entered and—sure enough—the two SAS men were there . . . stuffed with their own webbing.

All in all, Maude had had a field day. Apart from the brace of SAS lads, four plain clothes detectives, a Special Branch investigator, and a drum majorette were all sitting round a table, stuffed.

A general alert was sounded, and I returned to inform the Prime Minister that Aunt Maude was on the loose again. He was still at it:

'And furthermore, my fellow countrymen, let us strive at the next General Election, to give this party a bigger majority.'

I whispered to the producer, who in turn whispered to his floor manager, who whispered in the Prime Minister's ear and he went the colour of a Dulux primer.

The broadcast was hastily cut off and, after a furious discussion, Happy Daze was summoned to read a newsflash telling the populace that Maude was on the run. Hyde Park emptied like a faulty sluice, and soliders grabbed their weapons and milled around, firearms at the ready.

At Happy's request, I accompanied him and Nancy back to their place . . . We did not go alone. Several burly men went along with us, and I felt reasonably secure. We sat in the flat and had a cup of Bovril whilst Nancy finished messing about with an alderman. When she'd made him happy, she cut him down from the toilet cistern, took her nun's habit off, and joined us. The alderman bade us all a grave farewell, and booked an appointment for next Thursday.

I did not sleep at all well that night. I kept dreaming that Maude had me naked on a clothes line, and she was opening my stomach and shoving sawdust inside me. I cried out once, and awoke in a sweat. Nancy popped her head around the door, saw my discomfiture, and got on the sofa with me. Within minutes, I was being manhandled into a realm of physical ecstasy . . . The things that woman could do with oven gloves and lard!

The following morning, I checked on our security men outside; and, with relief, I found them animated and unstuffed. The telephone rang and it was answered by Nancy, who looked quite ravishing in her outfit of an Australian bush hat, leather truss and spats. She smiled at me as she picked up the receiver, but the smile soon faded.

'Oh no . . . not again,' said Nancy in a horrified tone. She held out the telephone to me as if it were a serpent. A voice, which I recognised as belonging to one of the Prime Minister's right-hand men, a slim ex-Harrovian with crimped curls and a perchant for wearing gaudy aprons and glass chokers, was speaking. 'For God's sake, make sure that peculiar man Daze is in Regent's Park tonight. Aunt Maude was spotted behind the lion house about an hour ago. The whole zoo area has been cordoned off and, hopefully, she'll be nabbed tonight. Oh, and by the way, she's been at it again . . . She's stuffed the entire Hallé Orchestra.'

As I replaced the receiver, I turned and saw Happy Daze standing behind me, wearing a sick expression and loud pyjamas. 'I'm fed up with being a bait for that nut,' he said weakly. I tried to reassure the poor devil, but I didn't sound very convincing; I was sure in my heart that he too would eventually finish up in the Ealing Warehouse. He threw himself on the sofa and sobbed like a dervish with athlete's foot.

Nancy's bedroom door was ajar, and I caught a tantalising glimpse of her spanking a man's bare bottom with a fishing rod. He seemed to be enjoying it and at one stage, he blew a feeble chord on a clarinet.

The newspapers were full of Aunt Maude and her escapades. Germany had broken off diplomatic relations with Britain, and in Munich a taxidermist had been lynched by a party of conservationists. I lit yet another cigarette and wondered when it was all going to end.

HAPPY DAZE performed in Regent's Park that evening, and on the bill was a very fine impersonator, one Mike Yarwood. He would have been magnificent, I'm sure, but unfortunately

Maude had got to him first and the poor lad was now a chunk of well-stuffed meat. He'd been disembowelled and crammed with Max Factor Cleansing Cream and talcum powder.

There was, of course, a bit of a panic: a young soldier wildly fired his rifle into a clump of dwarf oaks and shot a peeping tom up his anus; every old lady was rounded up, stripped and searched by grim vigilantes. All the old dears had delighted smiles on their faces—one of them was heard to shout, 'That hasn't happened to me since Verdun!' Crowds tried to surge out of the park and there were scuffles with security people and police, while a traffic warden had his teeth stolen. Anarchy ruled that night, and there was still no sign of Aunt Maude.

I found Happy Daze in his dressing-room, a BBC caravan. He was alone except for Mr Billy Cotton, who sat on the toilet with his trousers around his knees and a batch of *Radio Times* sticking out of his ears and nose. He was quite dead. Daze was in a state of shock, and I had to shake him violently to get him out of what appeared to be a cataleptic condition. Finally, he was coherent enough to blurt out the details of the latest outrage.

Apparently, he (Daze) had been taking off his make-up and the remains of a tomato that someone had hurled at him, when Mr Cotton had entered the caravan complaining of dysentery, brought on by looking at the latest TV ratings. He had gone into the lavatory, and must have failed to see Aunt Maude already sitting on the pan. Happy said there was no indication of violence, only the sound of knitting-needles clicking away and a muttered, 'You naughty man, invading a lady's privacy. I don't know what the world is coming to, I really don't!' Bill Cotton had said he was sorry, and what was the lady doing to him?

'You didn't see Aunt Maude go in the loo?' I demanded of Happy.

He shook his head, and pointed to a half-empty bottle of gin. 'I'd had a few to steady my nerves,' he stammered. 'I remember rolling on the bed, pissed, and I think I fell off into the corner of the caravan.'

It all fitted, of course. Maude had tracked Happy down

and had failed to see her protégé's inert figure lying on the floor, otherwise Daze, too, would have been an empty shell by now. Police and Army brass hats, armed men and tracker dogs, converged on the area around the caravan; they milled in ever-decreasing circles and condemned each other's tardiness in grabbing the potty Aunt.

A week rolled by. Still Maude remained undetected, and the indiscriminate stuffings continued. In two days she managed to stuff the Luton's Girls Choir with charcoal and kirby grips; four Jesuits from Florence on a pilgrimage to Huddersfield; a circus freak with a drink problem, and a Jewish florist in Tooting, who ended up in a clump of groundsel brimming to his tonsils with bagel crumbs. A Boeing at Heathrow was grounded for an hour when the flight engineer turned up in a sump with dusters rammed up his evacuation area, and on the television show 'Mr and Mrs', Derek Batey talked to a couple from Pontefract for over fifteen minutes before he realised they were both stuffed.

Oddly enough, at the United Nations, Britain was gaining respect, because most of the leading countries in the world firmly believed that we possessed a devastating weapon, and they put the reports of Aunt Maude down to typical British daft humour. The Arabs gave us free oil and allowed the export of Brown Windsor Soup to be resumed. China decorated Hong Kong for us and sent the Queen a free bag of jasmine tea, and Spain turned Benidorm into a site for Pontin's. We were becoming a nation to be feared with justifiable reason, for Maude, our beloved but insane human taxidermist, was stepping up her gruesome activities.

The audience for the opening night of the controversial sex film, DEEP THROAT, at a cinema in Harlow—with the exception of a two-year-old bassett hound in the foyer—was all stuffed with French nougat and cashew nut kernels. The whole team of 'Blue Peter' was unearthed in a cellar in Woking, and Happy Daze took over the programme and then ran like hell to introduce 'Tomorrow's World'.

It was in late August that the most awesome aspect of the whole business occurred . . . A cult sprang up calling themselves 'The Apostles of Maude'. Their belief was that the giddy old aunt was in fact the Fourth Prophet, and that when the world's population was stuffed, there would be no more war, nuclear weapons, famine or disease—which really, I suppose, did make sense. The cult grew and one was often accosted in the streets of any town by strange chanting figures in torn cardigans and flowery hats, handing one leaflets about the Coming of Maude.

Every night school, adult education centre and community hall in the land was giving lessons in taxidermy; and before long, cats stopped mewing, and the only dogs that moved were battery-operated. Politicians started jumping on the bandwagon and, in their ceaseless search for votes, gave full support to the Apostles of Maude.

Convicted murderers were offered the choice of life imprisonment or judicious stuffing for display purposes; Britain was going mad as well as broke, and there was a dire shortage again of toilet paper. It had to stop. In September, the Army took over the running of the nation, and the Royal Family were put in the Tower for their own safety.

No one any longer cared about Happy Daze; and in early December, Aunt Maude spirited him away. On Christmas Eve the untalented man was found in a grotto on the fourth floor of a department store. He was sitting on a sleigh with antlers on his head, and the poor chap had been stuffed with mistletoe and a dash of marzipan. He looked quite at peace and the window dressers left him there as he was, apart from creosoting his underpants.

With the death of Happy Daze, the stuffings stopped and the country started to get back to normal. The Apostles of Maude were rounded up and sent for training as Avon Cosmetic reps, and taxidermy was banned.

Because I was one of the few people who had actually met Maude AND lived to tell the story, I was asked to go on television and narrate the events. Overnight, I became a sort of personality and I wondered if I should take up juggling as well, just to break the monotony.

Nancy was delighted with my new-found success as a TV

chat-show personality, and we began to share the late Happy's bed—when she wasn't busy of course, with clients. Looking back now, although I found Nancy's work depressing, I realise it was one of her regulars who got me to Hollywood.

Perhaps I should go into more detail.

This man was a film producer who'd always been unlucky with his choice of movie titles. For instance, he had directed a great motion picture called 'Gone with the Breeze' and another monumental flop of his was 'All Quiet on the Eastern Front'. He tried musical pictures—he'd completed one called 'The Noise of Music', closely followed by 'Singing in the Sleet'. He was a short fat man with a huge, domed bald head and Nancy used to dress him up in plastic sheets and pour Oxo all over him. He always enjoyed it; Nancy would don her Long John Silver outfit for him, and he paid for his pleasure with a Diner's Club card.

One night, Nancy had overbooked and she was busy tying up a farmer in the linen closet, so she asked me to take care of her Hollywood tycoon. I didn't mind—there was nothing on the telly except mass auditions to get show business going again—so I wrapped him up in plastic sheets, poured the Oxo over his prostrate form, and dressed myself up as Quasimodo. I got carried away in the role and forgot to tickle his bald head with a goose claw. He didn't mind at all and—after he'd had his pleasure—he gave me a hefty tip, then invited me to go back to America with him, and try my hand as an actor.

That night, the producer and the farmer sat in knickers and pith helmets, Nancy in her 'Flicka the Wonder Horse' costume, while I was the Hunchback of Notre Dame, and we had a bit of a do with ginger beer shandies and watercress sandwiches. Three weeks later Nancy and I sailed for the New World.

MY CAREER in Hollywood started off very badly indeed. The only film work I could get was that of stuntman. In just one month—for a pittance, I might add—I was blown up in a bird sanctuary, tossed into a pit of sulphur by Tarzan, and eaten alive by a rampant baboon. Nancy did all right, though, and we moved into a tiny Beverly Hills apartment with a disused sauna shed in the attic, where she commenced her operations again. I was able to help her by supplying costumes from the studio wardrobe; her favourite was that of a Zulu foot specialist, and her clients loved her in it. (Our little producer was sacked from the studio after making a disastrous movie about the Mafia called 'The Godsister', he gassed himself at a friend's house to keep his bills down.)

Chance is a strange thing; I did a small part in a picture about a homosexual werewolf who falls in love with a painting of Shirley Temple then, in a fit of depression, swallows a candle. I had only a few words to say as I gagged on the tallow before hurling myself into a swamp, but when the picture was released, I got very good press notices. And, when the film went to England, I started receiving fan mail from Blighty . . . including a letter from Miss Amy Pluckett.

The Institution
Miresea-on-Crouch

My Dear Mr Dawson,

They let us see your picture in the Home, and you were wonderful in it. (Is Lassie queer?) Things have settled down here in Britain—there is no sign of Maude, and the danger is over. I think she's dead, you know, all that travelling she did.

Dr Snow is now a patient with us, and he's very nice, and Sir Peregrine Potts-Belching is his best friend.

All of us here are now fans of yours. Of course we remember what we tried to do for my poor nephew, Happy Daze, and that helps. One of your biggest fans is a new cleaning lady we have. She's very nice and she thinks so much of you, bless her, she said she'd like to save up and visit America. (Is Tarzan well hung?) Dr Snow thinks the world of her and lends her books on plastic surgery. (Isn't she clever? And she only comes from Watford.)

Must go now for treatment. (No . . . I'm not a teapot any more.) Look after yourself and good luck.

Amy Pluckett

Amy Pluckett (Your friend)

132

I don't know why, but the letter made me most uneasy; a familiar chill crept up my neck hairs. But when I voiced my fears to Nancy, she merely laughed and resumed massaging porridge on her client's genital area. She looked lovely, dressed in her Cherokee feathers and jackboots, and I longed to embrace her—but I can't stand porridge.

I was offered a small part in a film starring Rock Hudson to play, oddly enough, Quasimodo, the Hunchback of Notre Dame. It was an unusal story line based on the discovery that Quasimodo hadn't died in Paris but had been deep frozen in a lake, and brought to America as an exhibit. When thawed out, he falls in love with a good-time gal, portrayed by Racquel Welch, who is in love with Brick Mason, played by Rock Hudson, who is mad about a lapsed nun, played by Rita Hayworth.

It took hours for me to put the make-up on—and all my role involved was jumping up and down in a cage, and getting boiled in a tank of custard. It wasn't much of a part, but it came in handy. Rock Hudson, normally a first-class performer, started to get edgy on the set—especially with me. He would storm off the set, screaming and shouting, and things came to a head when he smacked my hump with a mallet. That night I heard him talking to himself. I knocked on the door of his dressing-room, and he stood there glowering at me. 'Mr Hudson,' I said nervously, 'I don't know what I've done to offend you, but I'm sorry for whatever it is. Perhaps I'd better leave the picture.'

He wept at my words and motioned me to sit down, and wordlessly, he handed me a soiled letter.

MY DEAR ROCKY,
    ALTHOUGH I LIKE YOUR FILMS, LES DAWSON IS A BETTER ACTOR THAN YOU. AND ALTHOUGH HE'S FAT AND SMALL, HE'S BETTER LOOKING, I THINK. SO GET OFF THE FILM NOW OR I'LL HAVE TO DO SOMETHING ABOUT IT.

The letter was of course unsigned. 'I've received one of these twice a week, sometimes more often. What the hell do you know about it? Tell me, have you been sending them?' Hudson's fist was clenched with anger as he spoke.

I reassured him that it was not I and that, in my opinion, it was the work of a crank; but I advised him to get a body guard just in case. He merely laughed and shoved me, goodnaturedly, outside.

The following day, when we all reported for work, I'd spent three hours getting my make-up on and I was tired and fed up. Rock Hudson did not show up in the morning, and at four o'clock in the afternoon we were dismissed. I tried his dressing-room door, but it was locked and I was about to leave when I heard a moan coming from inside. I ran back to the set and summoned the studio police, thinking that perhaps he'd had an accident. They burst the door down—I stepped back at what I saw, and screamed . . . Rock Hudson was sitting on his bed, and he had changed into the Hunchback of Notre Dame.

The doctor who examined the film star was as white as a frosted lawn. 'I don't believe what I'm seeing,' he gasped. 'Rock has been given plastic surgery, and a silicone hump has been sewn into his back.' Hudson tried to speak, but his twisted mouth made him very inarticulate and the only word I could understand was 'Bells'.

The studio had to hush it up and Rock Hudson was put under a close guard. The studio boss was nonplussed. 'Jeeze,' he spat, 'I gotta flick to do and no star. Aw, shit.' I felt sorry for him and, without realising it, spoke the first line of the dramatic scene in which Brick Mason finds Quasimodo rinsing his feet in a bucket . . . 'That this should be the soul of man.'

The producer squinted at me. 'Jeeze, another Humpy guy! Say, that line was okay, kid . . . Wait a minute, a star is born, get it? From humps to stardom overnight . . . What's yer name, Limey? Yeah, yeah, Dawson, get that make-up off and get ready to take a screen test. Youse is gonna take Rocky's place, baby.' That's how it happened. That motion picture made me a major star while Rock Hudson won an Oscar playing the Hunchback. One newspaper described his appearance as, 'The most fantastic make-up job ever.' If only they could have known at the time!

I was in a terrible dilemma: I knew beyond all reasonable doubt that Aunt Maude was at it again, but who would believe me? The studio promoted the story that Rock Hudson had retired from the industry, and was concentrating his time on UNICEF. In actual fact, he'd gone slightly dotty and run off to Rangoon with a midget.

A big studio publicity party was held in the 'Pump Room' of one of Hollywood's better hotels. Fans besieged the place and what with the speeches and the wine, I was, to put it bluntly . . . knackered. It was late when I got back to the apartment, which Nancy and I were leaving for a bigger place the following week. I wearily entered, and threw myself on to the bed but awoke with Nancy tugging my shoulder urgently.

'Wake up, for Christ's sake, ' she yelled. 'We've got to do something bloody quick . . . the old fart's been here.'

I jerked myself away from the mattress and saw Nancy panting in the doorway. She had an expression of horror on her face, which appeared slightly ludicrous, because she was dressed as Joan of Arc. She hustled me up into her attic, and there, lying on the bed, was another Quasimodo; hump, twisted mouth, the lot.

'Oh, my God,' I uttered. 'Who the hell was he?'

Nancy burst into tears. 'That used to be Kirk Douglas!'

She poured out the entire story. Kirk Douglas had very recently been introduced to her, though not for aberrational sex; he merely wanted to put her nose in his cleft chin while he played a mouth organ. She had let Douglas rest between numbers and had gone to pay a house call on an invalid who like his knees ironed as she sang hymns. When she returned, she'd found the actor remoulded—he was in a terrible state, and he'd lost his cleft chin.

The FBI came to the flat and Kirk Douglas was hustled away to a private clinic to join Rock Hudson, who had been expelled from Burma. I was getting some mighty queer looks off the Federal agents, and it would be only a question of time before my involvement with Aunt Maude came into the open. But in a trigger-happy society such as the Good Ole' USA, the thought of casually informing the CIA, the FBI and all other sundry security groups that the same old lady was responsible for the outbreak of Quasimodos, just as she'd caused the stuffing outrage in Britain . . . Well, no, thanks.

I started work on a low-budget movie called 'The Thing From Under The Rug', in which I was billed second to Lee Marvin. We began shooting in April and, by the middle of that month, Lee Marvin was another Quasimodo. Someone picked up the leads pointing to me, and I was taken away to FBI headquarters.

I was grilled under hot lights for hours, and finally, after being made to eat six cheeseburgers, I broke down and told them the whole story.

To say that the FBI men were amazed is, I suppose, something of an understatement. Nancy was summoned to testify on my behalf, and she arrived as 'Cleopatra Of The Nile', looking stunning. She, too, was subjected to interrogation, and finally the grim-faced agents believed us.

Al Bronco, a hard-bitten Federal Agent, puffed heavily on his cigar. 'Jesus H . . . We've got a nut loose and three friggin hunchbacks . . . Joe, we gotta phone MI5,' he breathed. As he was speaking a man dashed in and whispered to him and they turned and gazed at me with something akin to dread. 'Jesus H Bronco said in an almost reverent tone. 'They picked up Charlton Heston on the freeway . . . The old dame's done the job on him . . . now he'll never get a Biblical role again. And my wife loved the guy as Moses.'

MI5 reluctantly admitted that Britain had undergone the agony of Old Maude and the pound dropped ten cents.

News that I was to be deported threw Maude into a postive frenzy. Within the week, she had made Quasimodos out of Mickey Rooney, Marlon Brando and Robert Mitchum . . . They duly joined the others in the clinic; to pass the time away, the affected actors formed a rep company and put on a musical version of The Hunchback Of Notre Dame for charity. The hit song was 'Put On A Happy Face'. It was such a success that several bit players volunteered to undergo surgery to become a Quasimodo, and a song called, 'Over

My Shoulder Goes One Hump' rocketed up the charts.

The search for Maude was intensified, but it was kept from the American public for fear of Ronald Reagan going back into pictures. The night before Nancy and I were due to be booted out of the States, I read the headlines in the *New York Times* telling of the resumption of the cold war with Russia—I went to bed and had a dream, which led to a crackpot solution.

I gave Al Bronco my idea, he gave it to somebody else and the next minute, I was being flown to the Pentagon. General Ludwig P. Kolowsky had been an all-American Boy at Yale and his exploits in Vietnam were legendary. He stood six feet seven, didn't smoke or drink, and ran up frocks for his mother. He was the father of two strapping sons who were now at West Point, and his wife had piles. When he shook my hand, it was like caressing a turbot and he tended to spit when he spoke. Again I explained my plan for ridding the country of Maude, and he slapped his mighty hams and roared: 'Great kid, that'll teach the bastards.'

Three nights later, as per the plan, I went on the Johnny Carson show . . .

Johnny Carson had been briefed as to what was to happen, and he looked at me as if I should be on my way to a rubber cubicle. 'Is this a gag?' he asked Al Bronco. Instead of replying, Bronco merely let him see a letter from the White House. Carson paled. 'Shit,' he said.

It was obvious that Carson was still a wee bit sceptical, until General Kolowsky took him on one side and divulged most of the story, and Carson said, 'Shit,' again.

On the Carson show with me was a very great actor indeed—Cary Grant, whom I looked forward to meeting. I did, but not under the best of circumstances, because Maude had met Mr Grant first in his dressing-room, and he was now a very handsome seventy-odd-year-old Quasimodo.

Urgency was the keynote—we had to get rid of Maude.

After Grant had been hustled away to the clinic on the end of a rope, the studio was sealed off tight. The show began:

Carson: 'Hi everybody and welcome to the show . . . and you're welcome to it.' (*Hoots from audience.*)

Dawson: 'Hi Johnny, nice to be here.' (*Roars.*)

Carson: 'You've certainly had an up and down career in America, Les, from stuntman to star and then threatened with deportation after the disappearance of several big movie idols.'

Dawson: 'Yes, very worrying, but everybody knows now that I'm innocent. It was just one of those strange things, but many big names who vanished are, it seems, working for UNICEF.'

Carson: 'I heard a rumour that Rock Hudson was going to play Quasimodo?' (*Peals of laughter.*)

Dawson: 'He did, and lost three dollars.' (*Shrieks.*)

Carson: 'That must have given him the hump.' (*Hysterics.*)

Dawson: 'I think you're right, that's my hunch.' (*Screams.*)

Carson: 'Ha ha ha . . . There is nothing like a Notre dame.' (*Too much.*)

Dawson: 'His wife would have hit him but Esmer held her.' (*Total collapse.*)

We stopped gagging and, out of the corner of my eye, I saw General Kolowsky and Bronco glaring at me. I knew what the next question was, and I prayed that Aunt Maude was watching the show.

Carson: 'Seriously though, is it true that you are going to Soviet Russia on a cultural tour, and that you are going to play Long John Silver?'

Dawson: 'Yes, but there is strong opposition from the Russian government and actors over there who say that they can do it much better than I.'

Carson: 'Well, we wish you good hunting, Les.'

The commercial break came in, and I was taken off the studio floor and I received a big hand from the audience. I looked at Kolowsky and said that I hoped it had worked; Carson was told to keep his mouth shut and Bronco broke wind.

Two months went by and, although I played in other films, no actor was turned into Quasimodo. It began to look as if my plan had worked. All flights to Russia were monitored by the FBI and at last we received word that an elderly lady had been spotted aboard a plane at Kennedy Airport. She had given the name 'Miss Maude Daze' and I knew it was the deranged aunt. Nancy and I left America and came back to London, where we bought a large house, with a garden, in Notting Hill Gate with a big cellar that would come in handy for Nancy's brand of expertise.

For my part in getting Maude to go to Russia, I was given the American Congressional Medal Of Honour, the Purple Heart and free tickets to Disneyland. I was also taken to a room in the War Office and secretly given a medal and a fortnight's holiday in Malta. Miss Pluckett was allowed a welding set in her room, and Nancy was permitted to advertise in the *Guardian*.

Vague reports filtered in suggesting that Aunt Maude was having a wonderful time. The entire Bolshoi Ballet company were all a leg short now, and the Russians had bought a forest in Norway and were frantically making wooden crutches for their Red Army. A Russian submarine was found beached at Flamborough Head, with a crew who hopped ashore to ask for political asylum and National Health legs. The Cold War was over and exports from this country to Russia in plastic kneecaps reached an all-time high.

Well, there you have it—the full story as it happened.

Nancy and I have settled down very well; as I pen these last words, I can see her in the garden looking quite ravishing in her King Neptune outfit. She's chasing one of her clients, an unfrocked Rabbi, with a pair of shears and a papier mâché lance. My life has changed for the better, and it's all thanks to Miss Pluckett, Happy Daze and yes . . . Dear Aunt Maude. I often wonder what she's doing and where she is now.

Ah! It's time for tea! Here comes our lovely old housekeeper with a tray; she's a treasure, marvellous for her age, and we get on very well with her. Soon it will be time for Nancy and me to take our evening walk and talk about our adventures together, and perhaps to discuss the television commercial I've been offered. A company calling itself Toothy Bright Toothpaste have asked me—and for a lot of money, I might add—to make a film extolling the virtues of their product. I do have nice teeth so I might accept, although I was told that other actors would be doing similar adverts for rival brands of toothpaste, and the competition would be tough. Well, as I have said, things are back to normal, and Britain is doing pretty good . . .

Sorry, I had to laugh—but on the radio news just now was a story about Richard Burton being found without any teeth in his head, ha ha ha . . . Stupid, isn't it?

From Nancy La Tour to Amy Pluckett

Notting Hill Gate

Dear Amy Pluckett,

I knew your nephew very well indeed and I often go to see him in the grotto on the fourth floor of the big store in Regent Street. Even with the antlers on, he does have a certain dignity.

At present, I'm living with the writer Les Dawson—who of course you know—and, Miss Pluckett, I'm worried out of my head about him. I think Aunt Maude is back again and she's after him, I'm sure of that. Les was asked to audition for a television commercial for toothpaste, and he really thought he'd got it—which surprised me because his few remaining teeth are like condemned flats.

As you know, Les is small and very fat and not at all good-looking. Frankly, the only thing I'd let him model is a sheep-dip tank. When he went for the commercial casting I knew he wouldn't get it, but he was full of himself—and he can be a cocky little bleeder. When he came home, his face was dark with anger and disappointment, and he simply threw himself on the bed and drummed his heels.

I was busy with one of my clients, a cardinal from Cyprus, and so whilst I finished off putting axle grease up his nose, I asked our dear sweet housekeeper if she'd make our Les a cup of Marmite or something. She enquired if he was feeling all right and, rather impulsively, I told her that he'd lost the commercial. He wasn't good enough, for a start, and he'd been up against major actors like Robert

Morley and Roger Moore who were also auditioning. She seemed concerned and scurried away.

Then I forgot all about the housekeeper because, after the cardinal had left, I had another client—Chief Inspector Munche, who likes to be tickled as he sits on the gas meter. After he'd put his clothes back on and handed me my suspender belt (he wears it round his ankle during his climax) he told me that he was working on a very strange case indeed. Apparently the actor, Richard Burton, had been put to sleep and his teeth had been pulled out. After the inspector left, I went looking for my housekeeper, but she was nowhere to be seen. I found myself in her room, a tiny attic alcove, and I saw a blue scrapbook on a table.

The book was full of photographs of Happy Daze and Les Dawson. Pencilled in the margins were various remarks, such as: 'Dear Happy at the Palladium . . . Tommy Cooper won't be there!' On another page, was a picture of Tommy Cooper after he was found stuffed. There was a photograph of Les too . . . 'Dear Fatty Dawson, a lovely actor. Don't worry, darling, Kirk Douglas won't bother you.'

Yes, Miss Pluckett, you've guessed—there was a picture of Kirk Douglas. But not as we know him—he was the infamous Quasimodo.

Suddenly, I knew who our cosy lovable housekeeper was . . . Aunt Maude. I nearly wet myself with fright . . . I examined the other pages in the scrapbook, and there it was: a cutting from the evening paper saying, 'Richard Burton, approached to film a commercial for Toothy Bright, an up-and-coming toothpaste manufacturer.'

I rummaged through the chest of drawers and my fears worsened . . . I found instructions for plastic surgery, do-it-yourself brain operation kits, and . . . *Dentistry Made Easy*.

That was enough for me, Miss Pluckett, I telephoned the studio doing the commercial to warn them . . . Too late, Roger Moore had been made gummy and Robert Morley wasn't answering his 'phone. Disguising my voice, I rang the police and said that I feared for Robert Morley's safety. In the evening paper, to my horror, I read that Robert Morely had been discovered in his bath in a bemused state, and he had no teeth. Oh, Miss Pluckett, what am I to do? Maude hasn't come home yet, and I daren't have the police round here. They might find the rack and the chains and the other things that I need . . .

May I come and see you?

Nancy La Tour

Nancy La Tour.

Extract from Dawson's letter to the publisher

The Monastery
Somewhere near Scotland

. . . I realise that you find it very peculiar, having to leave my royalty slips
in a canvas bag on a wall in Cumbria, but that is the way it must be until
Aunt Maude is captured. When a man gets a commercial simply because
no other actor has any teeth, it's time to bloody well chuck it in.

Poor Nancy, when I found her in the kitchen trying to suck a
frankfurter with her ravaged gums, I knew there and then, that I had to
do something, and as you are well aware, I did. On the Michael Parkinson
Show, I condemned Aunt Maude soundly and although the studio
audience laughed like buggery, and Parky fell off his chair with mirth, I
knew that I had put myself in bad books with Maude, and how right I was.

The following week she sent me a letter and in it she stated quite
openly that she was most annoyed and intended to do something about it,
and for good measure, threw in hints about 'Making the last Quasimodo
toothless and immortal', and that, my friend, means she intends to stuff
me into the bargain.

I'm happy here and the monks are very kind to me, although my hair
shirt irritates me and I can't get used to the prayer wheel, but I'm still
intact, without kapok up my bum. I hear that Nancy went ga ga after
losing her molars and it's a great shame, although Miss Pluckett informs
me that Nancy's still at it in the Institution at Miresea, and doing the
inmates a world of good. Please don't try to find me, just keep sending the
pennies; I can't spend it but I've got it stashed under a stone in the herb
garden and one day I'll have a ball . . . (No women here, no spirits, just
wine made from chives, and a dirty old friar who keeps feeling me.)

Must go, it's time for Vespers and cocoa, so until we meet once more,
I am Sir,

Obediently Yours

Bro.Joshua

Brother Joshua.

BESTSELLING HUMOUR BOOKS
FROM ARROW

All these books are available from your bookshop or news-agent or you can order them direct. Just tick the titles you require and complete the form below.

☐	THE ASCENT OF RUM DOODLE	W. E. Bowman	£1.75
☐	THE COMPLETE NAFF GUIDE	Bryson, Fitzherbert and Legris	£2.50
☐	SWEET AND SOUR LABRADOR	Jasper Carrott	£1.50
☐	GULLIBLE'S TRAVELS	Billy Connolly	£1.75
☐	THE MALADY LINGERS ON	Les Dawson	£1.25
☐	A. J. WENTWORTH	H. F. Ellis	£1.60
☐	THE CUSTARD STOPS AT HATFIELD	Kenny Everett	£1.75
☐	BUREAUCRATS — HOW TO ANNOY THEM	R. T. Fishall	£1.50
☐	THE ART OF COARSE RUGBY	Michael Green	£1.95
☐	THE ARMCHAIR ANARCHIST'S ALMANAC	Mike Harding	£1.60
☐	CHRISTMAS ALREADY?	Gray Jolliffe	£1.25
☐	THE JUNKET MAN	Christopher Matthew	£1.75
☐	FILSTRUP FLASHES AGAIN	Peter Plant	£1.25
☐	A LEG IN THE WIND	Ralph Steadman	£1.75
☐	TALES FROM A LONG ROOM	Peter Tinniswood	£1.75

Postage _____

Total _____

ARROW BOOKS, BOOKSERVICE BY POST, PO BOX 29, DOUGLAS, ISLE OF MAN, BRITISH ISLES

Please enclose a cheque or postal order made out to Arrow Books Ltd for the amount due including 15p per book for postage and packing both for orders within the UK and for overseas orders.

Please print clearly

NAME ....

ADDRESS ....

....

Whilst every effort is made to keep prices down and to keep popular books in print, Arrow Books cannot guarantee that prices will be the same as those advertised here or that the books will be available.